FEMME

MARSHALL THORNTON

KB
KENMORE
BOOKS

Chicago
2016

Published by Kenmore Books
Edited by Joan Martinelli
Cover design by Marshall Thornton
Image by markovka via 123rf

ISBN-13: 978-1534906969
ISBN-10: 1534906967

First Edition

I would like to thank my beta readers and dear friends: Joan Martinelli, Fernando Chavez, Roberta Degnore, Owen Lovejoy, Kayla Jameth, and, Valerie and Randy Trumbull.

"Be yourself; everyone else is already taken."
— Oscar Wilde

CHAPTER ONE

Oh my fucking Gawd! That was the first thing I thought. Seriously, it was. I rolled over in bed, looked straight into a stranger's face, and thought, *Oh my fucking Gawd!* Well, no, it was not exactly a stranger's face. The guy was a regular at The Bird—the bar where I worked—and I did know his name. Sort of. His name was Dog. His teammates on the bar's softball team—the Birdmen—called him Dog. Not his real name, obviously, so I kind of didn't know his name. Oh my fucking Gawd! I had sex with a guy named Dog! How the flying fuck did that happen? The whole thing was a sloshy blur. I could barely remember anything about the night before. I'd gone to work like I did every Sunday afternoon. I remembered serving drinks and then, well...

Suddenly, I realized my nose was running and I had to blow it. Which reminded me that I'd been coming down with a cold for almost a week— That was it! While I was working I'd taken two cold tabs. Maybe three. Possibly four. Then I got off work and started having shots. Just to clear my sinuses. Fireball. Yum. Holy shit, I roofied myself. Oh my fucking Gawd! I roofied myself and had sex with a guy named Dog!

I kind of, sort of, maybe remembered the sex. It was fabulous. Or maybe it wasn't. I either had amazing sex the night before with a guy named Dog or I had the most mind-blowing sex dreams about that same guy named Dog. Given that he was lying next to me and looked like he was probably naked under my extra fluffy comforter, I suspected I'd actually had fabulous, amazing, mind-blowing sex.

As quietly as possible, I reached over to my nightstand and eased out a tissue. I used it to wipe my nose, but then realized that wasn't going to be sufficient. I had to *blow* my nose. And I had to blow my nose without making a sound. I tried but completely failed, instead making a sound reminiscent of a duck being strangled.

Dog's eyes popped open. He twisted his head around and took in my bedroom. I'd done an excellent job on the room. The walls were an amazing eggplant and the ceiling a delicate sky blue. I'd gotten this gilt- and cream-colored French provincial bedroom set on Craigslist that was so tacky it was chic. For whimsy, I had a collection of mirrors on one wall and throw rugs shaped like various fruits on the floor. My bedding had a zillion thread count and there was so much down in my comforter, my pillows and my feather bed that it was like I'd just shot, slaughtered and plucked a gaggle of geese.

I was waiting for a compliment. Instead, Dog said, "I don't live here."

"What a relief! I hate it when people move in uninvited."

Actually, I might not have minded so much if he had moved in uninvited. He was cute in a lumbering, jockish sort of way. His hair was dark and clipped close, his eyes a soft, puppy dog brown. (Hmmmm, maybe that's where he got the nickname.) There was a swoon-inducing dimple in his chin and, though he had muscles and very broad shoulders, he also had a sexy, hairy, little belly going on. That was an interesting thought. Since he was currently covered by my comforter the only way I'd know anything about his belly was—

I reached under the blanket and ran my hand across his modest paunch. Yup, it was there. And it was still sexy as hell. And we'd definitely had sex the night before. I was about to move my hand lower and start something new—I mean, after all, if the sex was half as good as I half-remembered we should definitely do it again—but he pushed my hand away and said, "Hey. Don't do that."

"Sweetheart, don't get all excited and scream rape. We're in bed together naked. That implies a certain intimacy."

"You're that waiter from The Bird."

"Lionel. My name is Lionel."

"That's a funky name."

"Your name is Dog. Do you really think you have room to talk?"

"I don't remember last night."

"Pity. I only remember parts of it. Maybe if we try a reenactment it will come back to us?" He looked seriously worried. That offended me a little. Well, more than a little. "Don't look like that. Trust me, you had the time of your life."

"I don't, um, I don't do things like this."

"You don't have sex? That's sad."

"I don't have sex with strangers."

"Yes, it's so much better to have cheap meaningless sex with people after you've cultivated a relationship with them."

I couldn't understand why the conversation had taken such a distressing turn. We'd ended up in bed together and now he seemed worried that I might think him a slut. I didn't think he was a slut. I *knew* he was a slut. Or rather, I knew he'd been a slut at some point. No one was that good at sex without a great deal of practice.

"How did this happen?" He seemed confused. Unfortunately, he was super cute when he was confused.

"This happened because you walked up to me, threw your arm around me and said, 'Wanna fuck?'"

"I did not say that. I wouldn't."

"You did. Have you considered the possibility of split personality disorder?"

"I should probably go," he said. "Do you know where my clothes are?"

I sat up and looked around the bedroom. There were no clothes on the floor, not even mine. I'm sort of a neatnik. Well, not sort of. Absolutely. Pulling the comforter around me I got out of bed. Normally, with a trick I just wander around naked. I mean what's the point of modesty in that sort of situation? But Dog no longer seemed interested in me so I didn't want to let him know that I was basically at half-mast. I mean, it was morning for one thing. And I was in bed with a naked man for another. These things happen. Apparently, these things were also happening to Dog since he grabbed at the sheet as the comforter dragged it along, trying, somewhat unsuccessfully, to cover himself. He was far fluffier than I was. He was at full mast. Apparently, he liked me more than he wanted to. Well, that was his problem.

I sashayed out to the living room to find his clothes.

Crap. My head hurt. It hurt bad. My mouth was dry. My stomach queasy. It was Monday morning and this happened a lot. Hangovers, not hook-ups. Softball was great. The exercise was good, the friendship, the feeling of belonging, those were all great. The afternoon of shots and beer after each game were not so great. Fun, just a bad idea. That Sunday the Birdmen won their first and only game of the season. I'd hit a double in the second inning and later on a single that drove home a run, so damned if I wasn't going to celebrate. Of course, landing in bed with the swishy cocktail waiter from The Bird had not been part of the plan.

"What time is it?" I yelled, hoping he'd found my clothes. And hoping my hard on would go away before he got back with them. I did remember having sex, though I wasn't going to let on. And it had been good. Real good.

"Eight-thirty!" Lionel yelled from the living room.

So much for going to the gym. I needed to get home, get showered, get shaved, get dressed and get on the road by ten. Ten fifteen at the latest. My shift at the hospital began at eleven, and while administering stress tests all day long was not what I wanted to be doing, it paid for my truck and kept food on the table. I wrapped the sheet around me. It sort of covered my stiff prick, which wouldn't get soft. Then I went into the living room.

There's this idea going around that every gay guy in America has good taste. Nope, not true. For example, this Lionel guy had painted his living room red. Freaking red. And, to make matters worse, in the middle of it was a white velvet couch that looked like he'd dragged it out of an alley. Between the purple bedroom and the red living room the apartment was done up like some movie decorator's idea of a Texas whorehouse. I didn't even want to know what colors he'd painted the bathroom and the kitchen. With enough rooms the guy would use every color in the rainbow flag.

Lionel stood next to a rusted metal table with a glass top that looked like it belonged in someone's backyard.

He was blowing his nose. Really loud.

"I kind of have a cold," he said.

Crap, I thought, *he's infectious*.

"Did you find my clothes?" I asked. Obviously he'd found his own, he was wearing a bright turquoise pair of boxer briefs with a white waistband. He looked good in them, perky ass, flat tummy, nice package. He looked good and he knew it, too. He was *that* type.

"Yeah," he said. He moved and I saw my clothes sitting on the table, folded into a neat little pile.

"Why did you do that?"

"What?"

"Fold them."

He picked the stack up off the table and held it out to me. "I was being nice. Don't you like it when things are neat?"

"I didn't want my clothes folded."

"If neatly folded clothes offend you, I apologize." And just in case his words weren't snarky enough, his tone pounded the point home like a hammer.

"I'm not offended. You just didn't have to do that."

"Do you want your clothes or not?"

I reached out to take them and the sheet loosened and fell to the floor. Instinctively my hands went to cover my crotch and the stack of my clothes ended up on the floor with the sheet.

Lionel rolled his eyes at me. "You can't seriously be shy?"

"I just—I don't know. It's a reflex." I bent over and grabbed my clothes and covered myself with them. I turned to go back to the bedroom and get dressed.

"You're really going to walk away with that?"

"With what?"

He put a hand on his hip and winked at me as he said, "A hard man is good to find." His voice was funny when he said it. Like he had an accent. Except it wasn't an accent. He was impersonating someone but I had no idea who. Then I realized he was waiting for me to react.

When I didn't he said, "Mae West. Famous actress from the nineteen thirties."

"Uh-huh," I said. Why did he think I'd know who that was? And why did he think it was sexy?

"Sorry. Big movie buff. Remember?"

"Oh, right."

"So you *do* remember?"

"No."

"We talked about it last night. On the way—"

"I didn't drive here did I?"

"Of course not. I don't let people drive in the condition you were in."

"So you drove?"

"Oh, Gawd no! I don't let people drive in the condition I was in either."

"So how did we get here?"

"We walked. I live two blocks from the bar. You really were out of it, weren't you? You don't have to worry though, you're an absolutely adorable drunk."

"Gee, thanks." I tried again to leave and go get dressed in the bedroom, but my boner was stubbornly bouncing around underneath my wadded up clothes. *This is stupid*, I thought. The guy was obviously into me. And I was obviously horny. It was probably a bad idea to have sex with him, but I figured having sex with him the morning after counted as the same bad idea as the night before.

"So, you were trying to say you wanted to have sex. With the imitation, that's what you were trying to get at. Right?"

"When I'm good, I'm good. When I'm bad, I'm better." Same voice, just as bewildering. I had no idea what to say to that so I walked across the room and grabbed him by the dick.

CHAPTER TWO

"So, Lynette, are you going to see him again?" Carlos asked, while we were waiting for our drink orders.

"I have absolutely no idea," I said, though it was late Sunday afternoon the following week and I was pretty sure the softball team was due at The Bird any minute. I had not heard a word from Dog since the previous Sunday. No surprise. After a quick but memorable round two, he'd run out of my apartment so fast he'd forgotten to take my number. I would have friended him on Facebook, but the only name I knew him by was Dog. There was a picture of him on the Birdmen's Facebook page, but it was captioned Dog. Just Dog. Not even tagged. No help whatsoever. But it was a cute photo of him in his baseball uniform—well, really it was more a baseball shirt and a pair of board shorts—but it was still cute. Of course, I also checked Grindr, Growlr, Scruff and several other apps I'd never even heard of before giving up.

"You're cool as a coconut. You know perfectly well the team is coming in soon."

"It's cool as a cucumber, Carlotta. And, yes, Dog is going to be here this afternoon. Big deal."

"Dog! I just love that name. Did you do it doggie style?"

"None of your business." My drink orders were ready, so I wandered off to deliver them—trying not to think too much about what we'd done in bed the previous Sunday.

Located in Long Beach's gay ghetto on what is called "the stroll," a section of Broadway with five or six gay bars, The Bird was half restaurant, half bar. The brick was exposed, the bar mirrored, and the inner walls tastefully painted forest green. Every day there was a drink special made with top-shelf liquor, usually a concoction the bartender invented that was too sweet for anyone to have more than one. Those who tried often ended up in the restroom puking up everything they'd eaten for the last week. An attached restaurant served small, tasty bites of elegant food on tiny triangular plates.

It was called The Bird because somewhere along the way they'd gotten a ginormous gold eagle and mounted it on the wall above what was then the cigarette machine and was now the cash machine. The eagle glared down at the room, wings spread, caught in the moment of takeoff as a roomful of gay men sipped fruity vodka drinks, eyed each other—usually to no avail—while listening to an overly loud piano player.

It was a nice place. You stopped at The Bird to have just enough drinks that you didn't care how trashy the rest of the bars on the stroll were. And they were pretty trashy. A block further down was a place called The Pub, which tried to present itself as somehow British, but just managed to be sad. Maybe it was the soggy indoor-outdoor carpet. Beyond that was a place called The Shaft that made you feel like you'd accidentally time traveled back to the nineties as soon as you walked through the door. Even further down were the places you went if you favored super cheap drinks and unintelligible conversations with tweakers.

Sunday afternoons were crazy busy at The Bird. There was brunch in the morning, which, after several pitchers of mimosas, could easily turn into an afternoon of drinking. Then, of course, the Birdmen came in around four. And finally, Larry Lamour started at five-ish.

Lamour was an old-school entertainer, who played the piano and told off-color jokes. He wore loud caftans and hats that often featured plastic fruit. His following was devoted, showed up for every minute of his sets, and shouted out his punch lines before he could get to them. He was good-natured enough not to get offended.

It was almost four when I managed to corner Carlos underneath the bird. The bar was only half full, so we were able to take a quick break.

"So, is your cold getting better?" he asked. "Your face is hardly blotchy at all."

"My cold is gone and has been since Thursday."

"If you say so, Lynette."

"Do me a favor, okay, and use my boy name in front of Dog."

He gasped. "Lynette, you'd deny who you are for a man?"

"Carlos, you're the only one in the world who calls me Lynette and you'd gut me like a fish if you thought it would get you laid."

"You have no social graces whatever. There is nothing ruder than the truth. Why do you think so many people avoid it?"

I glared at him.

"All right. Lionel," he said, as though simply saying my name left a bad taste in his mouth. "You really like this guy, don't you?"

"It was just a one-night stand. But it might be worth repeating."

"That's what a relationship is. A one-night stand that repeats and repeats and repeats."

Just then, the softball team began to trickle in. They were still in their red-and-black baseball shirts, which had a giant-beaked bird sketched across the front. I recognized the first two who walked in; one was named Tim and the other, Fetch. I remembered hearing a story about Fetch being an outfielder whose skills weren't entirely up to par. They put him in right field or left field, whichever field got less action, and let him fetch the ball when it rolled his way.

Tim was short, red-haired and balding, while Fetch was tall, black and probably fielded a lot of questions about why he didn't play basketball instead of softball. Of course, if he played basketball his nickname would be Dribble—so much worse than Fetch.

"Hello, boys," I said when I went over to take their order. "What can I get you?"

"Hey, can we get a couple of Millers," Tim said,

"And two shots of Fireball," Fetch added.

"Sure thing. How was the game?"

"Five-four."

"We lost it in the ninth."

I was pretty sure that meant they lost the game at the end. Of course, I had no idea how you'd lose a game at the beginning or in the middle.

"How tragic," I said, as though I understood what they'd said. "I'll get your drinks."

I went back to the bar and ordered their drinks. Sitting in a row next to the service bar were three of our Sunday regulars. Bill and Phil, two guys in their late seventies who'd been coming to The Bird since it opened and could tell you about the days when you could pick up the occasional sailor from the long-closed naval base, and Linda Sue, a nice, heterosexual, broad-shouldered, former professional football player who liked to spend Sundays in ensembles of brightly patterned wrap dresses, strappy sandals and a severe pageboy wig all picked out by his wife.

As I delivered drinks to Tim and Fetch, three more players came in. One of them I didn't know. The others were a British guy named Simon and his friend Jack, who was sort of lumbersexual. Carlos swooped over to get their order.

Tim and Fetch were semi-arguing about the last election, agreeing stridently about who should and shouldn't have been nominated in the first place. I found politics almost as boring as sports. Probably because people acted the same exact boorish way about both. Fetch gave me a ten and said to keep the change.

"Um, it's twelve dollars," I said. The Bird was not cheap. He probably came in on Fireball Fridays when you could get a Fireball shot for a buck, instead of its regular two-fifty.

Tim gave me another five and I made change from the bank I kept in my apron. He pushed a single back at me, and I smiled and said "Thanks," even though it was kind of a crappy tip. The thing I've learned about tips is to just smile and move on. After four or five rounds, Tim wouldn't be able to see the denominations on the bills and his tipping would markedly improve.

When I turned around to go back to the bar, I almost ran smack into Chuckie Cooper, real-estate agent extraordinaire and the captain of the Birdmen. Standing next to him was Dog. I looked at Dog but he quickly looked away.

I turned back to Chuckie, who was probably fifty but desperately wanted to be twenty-five. He was always over-groomed and I imagined him sleeping with two inches of moisturizer on his face, a chinstrap and pink tape around his eyes.

"Can you get us a couple drafts and two shots of Cuervo?" Chuckie ordered, raking his eyes up and down me as though I was something to be stepped on.

I turned to Dog, hoping to be funny and said, "And what about you, sir? What can I get you?"

"That's for both of us," Chuckie said, not finding me cute at all. He pulled Dog over to the table with Tim and Fetch. Dog still wouldn't look at me. He was acting like I was a complete stranger. Worse than a stranger. A stranger would have gotten a smile, a please, a thank-you.

I got nothing.

###

The pockets of my grimy shorts were crammed full of tissues. Most of them used during the game. I'd taken the maximum recommended dose of cold meds and just wanted to go lie down somewhere. I was kinda miserable. And it didn't help that Chuckie had pulled into the alley behind The Bird and asked for a blow job. There was no way I was doing that. I mean, I had. Once, at the start of last season. But only because he looked like an older Tom Brady. But there was no way I was doing it again. Ever.

Right after I'd joined the team we'd gone out, had a few, and he asked for a blow job. It wasn't the first time in my life I'd been asked. It *was* the first time that was all that was meant. Usually, guys asked "How about a blow job?" as a way of starting sex. The blow job was part one of the whole package of sex. But when Chuckie asks for a blow job, that's all he's asking for. And all he's offering. To be on the receiving end. No turnabout is fair play. Later on, the guys on the team warned me about

Chuckie, and I acted like it was a big surprise. Like I'd dodged a bullet.

So when I walked into The Bird, I was kinda groggy, a little dizzy, needed to blow my nose, and felt sexually harassed. I didn't expect to run into Lionel first thing, and really hadn't wanted to run into him while I was standing next to Chuckie. I don't know why, but I didn't want Chuckie to know I'd slept with Lionel, so I pretended I didn't know him.

That wasn't very nice.

Chuckie pulled me over to hang out with Tim and Fetch, who'd grabbed a small, table and four stools. Even though we'd lost to the Mermen who played for Waves, the dance bar on Ocean, Tim had pitched a few good innings as relief and Fetch had caught two of the three flies that had come his way. That didn't keep everyone from being depressed by our loss.

"We've got to do something to shake things up," Tim said.

"Yeah, we can't keep losing like this," Fetch agreed. "It sucks."

Lionel brought our drafts and shots. What I really wanted was tea and honey, and a nice soft pillow, but that wasn't going to happen anytime soon. By that point, I was already up shit creek and I wasn't going to ask Lionel for a paddle. Or a hot toddy. He took Chuck's credit card and went back to the bar. I kept an eye on him while trying not to let him know I had an eye on him. There would probably be a point when I could go over and apologize. Maybe when the awful singer started his act. Or when Chuckie decided to go and harass someone else.

"How about the ass on nelly girl?" Chuckie asked the table. I glanced around the room, but the only woman there was in her sixties and the decade she'd spent on a bar stool had not done her ass much good.

"Who are you talking about?" I asked.

"Nelly girl. The cocktail waitress."

"Lionel does have a great ass," Tim said.

Fetch nodded enthusiastically.

They were nicer about it than Chuckie, but it still bothered me. I mean, they talked that way about guys all the time. Heck, I talked that way about guys. But for some reason I didn't want them talking that way about Lionel. Which was stupid because, well, because it was stupid.

"It's a shame an ass like that is attached to such a flamer. When I'm fucking a man I like to know it's a man," Chuckie said, then glanced over at me. "Why is your face so red, Dog?"

"I, uh, I have a cold."

"Did you just get it? Because your face wasn't this red in the car. You know, that is the same color red my father's face gets when he forgets to take his blood pressure medication. Dude, are you going to stroke out?"

"I'm fine."

"Really? Because I can have nelly girl call you an ambulance."

I turned and saw Lionel standing next to our table with Chuckie's charge receipt in one hand. I wasn't sure how long he'd been there. He'd obviously heard at least some of what Chuckie said. Setting the receipt onto the tiny table, Lionel kept his face very still. In fact, the whole table was still. Everyone seemed hyper-aware of how rude Chuckie was being, except Chuckie.

Lionel took a deep breath, got a little bit taller, and said, "Honey, you can call me anything you want if you'd only learn to tip."

"What did you say?" Now it was Chuckie getting red in the face.

"I said, 'You need to learn to tip.'"

"You know I'm good friends with Bob."

"Bob the owner or Bob the guy who cleans the urinal?" To the rest of us he added, "Bob the urinal guy, he does that for free. Gets off on it." He shrugged his shoulders up high. "To each his own."

"Bob Grottoli. The owner."

"Oh *that* Bob? You think you're friends with *that* Bob? Well...you may think you're friends with a lot of people but..." A dramatic frown. "Not so much."

"Oh snap," Fetch said. "He's got your number, Chuckie."

Anger dripping off him, Chuckie filled out the credit card slip. He handed it to Lionel. "You're the sort of faggy queen who gives the rest of us a bad name."

Calmly, Lionel took the slip and looked at it. "Zero tip. Why am I not surprised?" Then he flounced off. I mean, he made a point of flouncing. In fact, I'm not sure I'd ever seen anyone flounce until that moment.

Chuckie was talking about how well he knew Bob Grottoli and how he was going to have Lionel's job. I should have said something. I felt like an ass for just sitting there while Chuckie acted like an ass. I shouldn't have let him. I should have stopped him. I'd wanted to, but I'd choked. Actually, I almost did choke. There was a lot of phlegm in my throat.

On the other side of the bar sat a black baby grand piano. Larry Lamour, wearing a brightly patterned housedress and a hat depicting the universe: the crown painted yellow, six hat-pin planets in different sizes and a spray of stars shooting out of the middle of it all, sat down and started to play a song that was probably a hundred years old, something about a carriage and a bicycle built for two. I think Lamour had messed up the words, though, "Andy, Andy, give me your answer true.

I'm half randy over the thought of you..." I don't think the song was originally about a dude named Andy.

It seemed like a good time to make my move. I said, "Excuse me" to the table, and wandered off like I was heading to the men's room. I looked around for Lionel but didn't see him anywhere. I slipped out the back of the bar to the smoking area. He was there, leaning up against the back wall of the building smoking a cigarette.

"I didn't know you smoked," I said.

"I quit. I just keep forgetting I quit."

"Look, I'm sorry about Chuckie. He's an asshole." I took a ten-dollar bill out of my pocket and tried to hand it to him. He just kept smoking. "I shouldn't have let him say those things. I should have stopped him."

"Sweetheart, in case you didn't notice I can take care of myself. I don't need you to protect me. I'm not a damsel in distress."

"That's not, I didn't mean—you know he's probably going to try and get you fired."

He dropped his cigarette onto the ground and stepped on it. Then he rested a hand delicately on his chest and said, "When I was a little boy, my only dream was that I would someday serve drinks in gay bar. Please, kind sir, do not let that evil man crush my dream."

"You're not being serious."

"Of course, I'm not being serious. War is serious. Cancer is serious. Starvation is serious. Whether or not I work at The Bird? Not such a big deal in the scheme of things."

"You don't mean that. Look, go back in and buy him a drink. Say something that sounds like an apology and you'll be okay."

"He calls me names and stiffs me, but you think I should buy him a drink and apologize? Did you get hit in the head with a bat?"

"Come on, you are kind of a stereotype. You're not stupid, you know that."

"I'm a fucking stereotype?"

"I didn't mean it that way." I was sure there was a nice way to say what I wanted to say, I just had no clue what it was.

"No, that's fine. You meant it that way. And, yeah, I'm a fucking stereotype. Knock-knock, so are you. So is everybody. It's how we identify one another. It's how we communicate with strangers. Every single person is a stereotype until you get to know them. Getting to know someone you find out all the ways they don't fit their stereotype. You find out the other things they are, the stereotypes they've played and rejected. When I was a little boy, I was a mama's boy. That's a stereotype. Except my mother died when I was ten. So I was a mama's boy without a mama. No one knew what to do with that. Then when I was a teenager, I was very emo, borderline Goth, very Winona Ryder in *Beetlejuice*. That's another stereotype."

Winona Ryder? Was she that singer? He must have misread the confused look on my face because he kept going. "I know, I know, not even my generation. But the aughts suffered a real lack of teenage rebellion. I mean, I certainly wasn't going to model myself after Amanda Bynes. When I turned eighteen, my father had had enough of a depressed, semi-suicidal teenager and threw me out. Best thing that ever happened to me. I got a job as a bus boy. Went to beauty school. I know, a gay boy at beauty school. Stereotype. Then I realized no one wants to actually pay for a haircut anymore and I got a job working here. And, yes, I'm nelly, I'm femme, I'm a flamer, I'm a queen, whatever you wanna call me. But I'm me. And I'm good at being me."

"Okay."

"Okay? What does that mean?"

"I don't know. It seemed like what I should say. That was a lot of words."

"And your response is *one* word?"

"I'm sorry your dad threw you out. He shouldn't have done that."

"See, you're the strong silent type, that's a stereotype. And you're kind of a bear, that's another stereotype. And you're straight-acting. That's also a stereotype. Oh Gawd, why do I bother?"

He pushed off the wall and started to go back inside.

"Wait—" I said, then couldn't get anything else out. I was caught by the way his skin looked flushed in spots by anger, and the incredible blue of his eyes. He was sexy and I couldn't figure out exactly why. Yeah, he was good-looking, but the world is full of good-looking guys. And very few of them are sexy for more than a minute. Lionel struck me as the sort who'd be sexy no matter what he looked like.

Stopping, he looked back at me with a sort of leer, seeing exactly what going on in my head, and said, "Oh honey, that ship has so sailed."

CHAPTER THREE

Yes, yes, yes, I hear you, darling. I should have kept my big fucking mouth shut. The customer is always right. What does the occasional insult matter when it means I'm not living in an alley eating out of trash cans? Believe me, all of these thoughts crossed my mind as I walked home from The Bird. It also crossed my mind to wonder what the fuck I should do with my life.

I couldn't be a cocktail waiter forever. I knew that. But when you're on your own there aren't always many options. I mean, I was doing okay. I had a job. Well, hopefully I had a job. I had an adorable little apartment. I even had a thousand dollars saved in a CD to buy a car so I could stop begging people for rides. I had a pretty good idea how I wanted the next year of my life to go. Beyond that things were fuzzy.

Deftly, I managed to avoid Chuckie Cooper for the rest of my shift. Carlos was nice enough to take care of the Birdmen and their orders, so I didn't have to go near them. I dealt mainly with a swarm of older guys there to see Larry Lamour. Some of them were a bit handsy, which compared to Chuckie wasn't so bad. One of the older guys who comes in every week—I think his name is

Gilbert, though some people call him Coco—offered me a trust fund if I'd run off to Vegas and get married. Though, it was very loud by then so he might have said, "I think it would be *such fun* if we went to Vegas and got married." Not that I would do it. Cash or no cash. But it is always nice to be asked.

The Birdmen were gone by seven. Drifting off to other bars, or in a few cases patient husbands holding dinner. Because Carlos had been nice enough to run interference with Chuckie, I let him go home first. One cocktail waiter went home at eight and the other at ten. It was my turn to get off early, but Carlos always wanted to get home early and walk his dogs. One of them was old and there was a fifty-fifty chance she'd pee on the floor if left alone for more than an hour or two. Leaving her alone for a six-hour shift was hopeless.

"I think I saw Chuckie on his cell phone. He might have been talking to Bob."

"Carlotta, half the guys in the bar were on their cell phones at one point or another. Some of them were texting each other rather than getting up to walk across the room."

"Chuckie Cooper is not a nice man. You need to be careful."

When my shift ended, I could have wandered down the stroll for a drink at the Pub or some other place, but the last thing in the world I wanted to do was run into any of the Birdmen. So I walked home, planning to watch a DVD.

My building is an L-shaped, two-story stucco painted the color of cinnamon icing, surrounding a courtyard filled with old-growth birds of paradise and elephant ear ferns. There's a security gate that doesn't work, which is unfortunate since anyone could walk in. And anyone had. Dog sat on the narrow stoop in front of my first-floor apartment. He looked sad and his face was blotchy, like he'd been crying. *He hadn't been crying had he?* I worried. *That would be hideous.*

"I thought you had no memory of how you got to my apartment when you were here last week?"

"I was sober when I left. Remember?"

"And you left a trail of breadcrumbs."

"Why would I do that?"

"What are you doing here?" I asked. "Wait, don't answer that. I know why you're here. I told you. That ship has sailed. You're cute and I probably would have fucked you again, but now the whole thing is kind of ruined. Once I'm off the scent, I'm off. Got it?"

Suddenly, he sneezed. Hard. He pulled a rumpled, over-used tissue out of the pocket of his shorts and tried to clean up his nose.

"I gave you my cold, didn't I? Shit."

"I think the medicine I took is wearing off."

"So this isn't a bootie call, is it?" Or at least I hoped it wasn't. He couldn't be so arrogant he'd think I'd have sex with him while he was oozing mucus. Though, to be honest, he had had sex with me while I was—

"I want to ask you to dinner."

"Dinner?" Gawd, I sounded like I'd never heard the word. "You mean like a date?"

"Yeah. Why not?"

"Because it's a bad idea, that's why not." And it was a bad idea. I doubted we had anything in common. And even though I had a very pleasant moment imagining myself as Susan Sarandon in *Bull Durham* sitting in the bleachers at an imaginary ballpark wearing sexy off-the-shoulder sweaters while cheering on my baseball-playing man, he really wasn't my type at all. My type was more nerdy computer guys who could bore me for hours talking about the usefulness of algorithms or hipster-ish bisexuals who'd bring their girlfriends to The Bird to meet me. Okay, so maybe I've *never* had much in common with the guys I went out with, but still, Dog was just so—

"Wait, how long have you been sitting here?"

"Couple hours."

"You have a cold and you've been sitting at my door for a couple hours?"

"Yeah."

What kind of guy does that?

"Okay, fine, I can at least make you some tea and honey," I said, unlocking my front door. As soon as I said 'tea and honey' he got a ridiculously happy look on his face. Odd, to say the least.

He followed me in. As I closed the door behind him, I got a bit too close and smelled the beer he'd had and sweat from his game and a rather nice aftershave he'd put on many, many hours ago. It was a much sexier smell than I wanted it to be.

"So, do you have a history of mental illness?" I asked.

"That's not a nice thing to ask."

Waiting around for me like that was sweet, but not well thought out. "No, it's probably not a nice thing to ask. But it's a good thing to know."

"I'm fine. Would you have made me leave if I wasn't?" There was something defiant about his expression.

"No. But I'd ask you a lot of questions."

"I have the feeling you're going to ask me a lot of questions anyway."

That was probably true. I stepped into my miniscule kitchen and put the kettle on. When I returned, Dog was still standing in the middle of my living room. "You can sit down. It's okay."

"There's dirt on my shorts. I don't want to ruin your couch."

On the one hand, the couch was fabulous. It looked like something Liberace had owned in the sixties. On the other hand, I'd gotten it at Out of the Closet for fifty dollars. Still, I'd spent a whole week scrubbing it clean and deodorizing it. I went into the living room, grabbed a cherry red throw that matched the walls, spread it over the sofa and said, "Better?"

"Now I'll get your nice blanket dirty."

"Are you angling to take your clothes off?"

He blushed and sneezed.

"Let me get you a decent tissue." Leaving the room, I added, "And for Gawd's sake, sit down. The blanket is washable."

I actually didn't have any decent tissue, so I brought him his own personal roll of toilet paper from the bathroom and set it on the glass coffee table that belonged to a completely different era—fifties patio—but still managed to work with my couch. I watched him blow his nose, which he did in an oddly delicate way. When he was finished, I asked, "Why Dog?"

"My name is Doug. The first day of practice some of the guys heard me wrong. It stuck."

I was expecting something more interesting, but was kind of glad I didn't get it. "Well, that's better than a story about you peeing on a fire hydrant."

"They made me do that after the first game."

"Nice."

"They're good guys."

"Yeah, they're okay. I know most of them. I've been working at The Bird for two years."

A cloud seemed to pass over his face and I was afraid he'd bring up my apparently-hanging-by-a-thread job again. Fortunately, the kettle whistled and I scurried into the kitchen. Making his tea, pouring the water over the bag, getting out the honey bear, squeezing a big glob into the cup, and then adding a tiny shot of whiskey, I felt very domestic. My mom used to make me something similar when I was a kid, not as much whiskey but some. She'd whisper in my ear when she gave it to me, "Don't tell anyone." It was our secret.

Walking back into the living room, I wondered what I was doing. I had the sinking feeling I should never have invited Dog into my apartment.

###

Lionel hadn't answered my question, hadn't said whether he'd have dinner with me. He'd said it was a bad idea, but that didn't always mean no. It usually meant no, but not always. I needed to convince him that it was a good idea to have dinner with me. I just wasn't sure how to do that.

Or why? Why did I want to have dinner with him? I wasn't sure. I just did. I liked listening to him. I mean, I liked having sex with him, too. But that wasn't going to happen over dinner. It might not even happen after dinner. It definitely wasn't happening tonight. Not while I had a cold. Making out with someone while you've got a cold causes oxygen deprivation. Not fun.

Lionel handed me the tea. Except it was more than tea. It was half booze. *Well,* I thought, *maybe it will dry me out.* That and the three shots of tequila and four draft beers I'd managed to have at the bar. Oh, maybe that's why I wanted to have dinner with him. I was a little drunk. I did stupid things when I was drunk. Like having sex with Lionel in the first place.

No, that wasn't stupid. It had been nice. And I did it once when I was sober, too. It was even nicer sober.

"What?" I asked. Lionel had sat down in the bright yellow chair that looked kinda like a daisy. He'd said something but I had no idea what it was. Now he was staring at me. "What did you say?"

"I asked if you have a fever."

"Oh. No. It's just a cold. You only get a fever with the flu. Unless it's a respiratory infection. Or pneumonia. But this isn't. Either."

He looked at me very seriously and asked, "So darling, who are you? Exactly?"

"I told you, people call me Dog."

"And your name is really Doug. And you like softball. Tequila shots. Draft beer. There are certain things in the sex department you are very enthusiastic about, but I won't mention them because…" He watched me intently as my face flushed. "…you embarrass easily. The blushing is very cute by the way. All in all you're quite tempting. Tell me something that will make you more than tempting. Be irresistible."

I had no idea what to say. Or how to be— So, I said, "That's not fair. You're putting me on the spot."

He smiled a little as though he liked my answer. "What kind of job do you have? Why don't we start there?"

"I administer cardiac stress tests at Harbor."

"That sounds interesting."

"It's okay. It's a job."

"What kind of job do you really want?"

"I wanted to be an EMT, drive an ambulance, but that didn't work out."

"Why not?"

I took a big gulp of my whiskey tea. "I got a DUI when I was twenty. You can't get insured with a DUI so no one will hire you."

"Do you have a drinking problem?"

"Only on Sundays."

He nodded. "Why did you want to drive an ambulance?"

I shrugged. "I guess I wanted to save lives."

"And wear a uniform?" He added a sexy wink to that.

"It is kind of a cool uniform."

"Are you sorry that you're not an EMT?"

"Yeah, I guess."

"Well, listen sweetheart, the tests you give help save people's lives. And you're wearing a kind of uniform right now. You're not that far off from where you were aiming." He had a habit of waving his hands around when he talked. He saw me notice and laid his hands in his lap, one on top of the other. I didn't think he'd be able to keep them there long. "What else? Tell me your coming out story. That's always very revealing."

"I sort of dated women until I was twenty-one. I almost got married, but it never felt right. When I told my ex-fiancée I was gay she didn't believe me. She thought I was lying so she didn't feel bad about my dumping her."

"Saying you're gay to be polite, yeah, people do that all the time."

I shrugged. It was what she said. I couldn't help that.

"How are your parents about it?"

"They don't know."

"You're not out to your parents? How old are you?"

"Twenty-eight."

"I guess you have that option."

"What does that mean?"

"It means you're straight-acting." He used obnoxious air quotes around straight-acting. "People assume you're straight. I'm a sissy boy. No one assumes I'm straight. When I come out people roll their eyes and say, 'Big surprise.' Are you going to tell your parents? Or are you just going to wait for them to die?"

"My dad has a heart condition and he's kinda religious now." And I didn't want to see the disappointment in his eyes when I told him.

"But you know how to do CPR, don't you?" I must have made a face, because he immediately said, "Sorry, I suppose that wasn't very nice."

"What do you want to be...someday?" I almost said when you grow up which would have been stupid. He seemed a little younger than I was but he wasn't a kid.

Lionel thought about it for a minute and then said, "Safe. I want to be safe."

Huh? People didn't say things like that. They said, they wanted to be an architect, or a businessman, or a pilot. What did it mean if all you wanted was to be safe?

"You said your dad threw you out?"

"On my eighteenth birthday. He did at least wait until after cake and ice cream. I thought that was good of him."

"So you don't ever see him?"

"Once. At Walmart. He was standing in the automotive section. I don't have a car, though, so I couldn't see any reason to walk over there." His hands were floating around again in front of him. He saw me notice again, but this time instead of stopping he waved his hands around more. "Is the tea helping?"

"Yes, thank you. It's making me sleepy. And kinda drunk."

"Where do you live?"

"Over near the marina."

"So you drove?"

"No. The field is in Tustin. Chuckie gave me a ride."

"And then he ditched you?"

"I ditched him."

"How did you plan to get home?"

"Ask for a ride or call an Uber, I guess."

"You can stay here, if you want."

"I'm not really up for—"

Lionel made a frowning face. "On the couch. You can stay here on the couch."

Since I was too lazy and too sick to call an Uber, I said, "Okay."

"Good. I'm going to go put on something more comfortable and then we'll watch a movie."

"Do you have pay-per-view? There's a new *Batman* movie."

"There's always a new *Batman* movie. No, we're going to watch something that's actually good," he said, then left the room.

Whatever he thought was really good was probably going to be really bad. But it didn't matter. I was actually feeling comfortable on the couch. I kind of liked being there. Even the red walls were growing on me. They were kind of scary in the daytime, but at night they made things seem sort of warm.

I wasn't sure what I was doing. No, wait, maybe I was. I felt bad because Chuckie had been such an asshole. Taking Lionel out for dinner was a way to make it up to him. And if I got laid again in the process, that was okay, too. No harm no foul.

Of course, this wasn't working out the way it was supposed to. He hadn't agreed to have dinner yet and now he was taking care of me while I was sick. If I wanted to make everything up to him, it was going to have to be a really nice dinner. If I could just get him to agree to it.

Right then, he came out of the bedroom wearing pink bunny pajamas and carrying a blanket and pillow. He tossed the bedding onto the sofa and said, "You can take your uniform off. I'll even turn around if you want."

"You don't have to," I said and started taking off my baseball shirt. "You told me I shouldn't be shy, remember?"

"Yes, I remember lots of things."

Across from the couch sat an old armoire. Lionel opened it and there was a small TV, with a cheap, tiny DVD player beneath it. Every other spare inch of the armoire was filled with DVDs. Without looking back at me he said, "I'm into DVDs. I know it's weird. So old-school. But I don't have cable or pay-per-view or even Netflix. I just have my movies."

He turned around to catch me in my boxer briefs and wifebeater. He took a good long look and seemed to enjoy it. I don't know why, but I grabbed the blanket and wrapped it around me. That made him smirk and made me feel stupid.

"Do you like Joan Crawford?"

"Is she the one who has the brother named John?"

"No, that's Cusack. You don't know who Joan Crawford is, do you?"

I shook my head.

"Well, my dear, be prepared to have your world rocked. We're going to watch the most fabulous movie ever made, *Mildred Pierce*. The story of a woman whose child is the most evil daughter in the world and yet Mildred still loves her enough to confess to a murder she didn't commit. It's stupendous. My favorite kind of movies are the ones where women do bad things."

I had no idea what to say to that. Why would that be anyone's favorite kind of movie? But it didn't matter. He started the film and ten minutes later I was fast asleep.

CHAPTER FOUR

Oh my Gawd, he kissed me. The fact that nearly four hours later I was still daydreaming about it was utterly ridiculous. Seriously, we'd fucked. Twice. Why was I getting all worked up about a single kiss for heaven's sake? But I was. He slept for nearly ten hours on my sofa and when he woke up he said he was feeling better. I made him another cup of tea, this time without whiskey, and a bowl of Count Chocula. He barely finished either since he had to call an Uber and get to work.

Right before he walked out the door to wait at the curb for his ride, he grabbed me, pulled me close and leaned in. For the tiniest moment, I thought he might not kiss me, after all. But then he pressed his lips against mine. They were hard at first, tight, tentative, careful. But then they loosened, relaxed, as though they suddenly felt safe, as though they'd found home. He tasted of tea and chocolate cereal and toothpaste, since I'd let him borrow my toothbrush. I mean why not? We'd kissed the week before. It was practically the same thing, after all.

And, the smell of him. He'd showered but still wore his softball uniform, so he smelled of body wash and perspiration, grass and shampoo, sweat and old cologne.

And beneath all of that was a warm, doughy, sweet smell that was, I don't know what, maybe it was pheromones or hormones or some secret, wonderful smell that only he had. I couldn't get enough of it.

His tongue slipped into my mouth, teasing, tickling, coaxing. I flicked my tongue against his, then I pushed back, eased my tongue into his mouth, and prodded, examined, searched every tiny speck of it. When I was done I ran my tongue around the inside of his lips, around in a circle, it was a sensitive spot. He quivered and stepped back in surprise. I pulled him back to me, held him pressed up against me and wouldn't let go.

He's quite a bit more substantial than I am and I liked that. Big arms, big shoulders, big chest. I liked holding onto him. Liked moving him where I wanted him. Liked when he pushed back. He's not much taller than I am, but he is wide and thick. Very much a ballplayer's body. Well, the one's I'd seen on the news. Or on the Internet.

The night before, after Dog fell asleep, I went and got my tablet. While still watching the movie, I looked up the rules to softball and found some pictures. The pictures were far more interesting than the rules. The good players were usually stocky, broad, sexy guys. That might not have been my type before, but it was well on its way to becoming my type.

Dog pushed away from me, stared at me closely with a questioning look, like he'd been surprised by the kiss— I'd certainly been surprised by it—then said, "I'm taking you to dinner whether you say yes or not."

"Dinner and a kidnapping. What more could a girl ask for?"

I saw him hesitate, briefly, maybe because I'd just called myself a girl. But then he plunged onward.

"Tomorrow night?"

"Sure. I don't have to work until Thursday."

"Good. I'll be here after my shift. Between seven thirty and seven forty-five."

And then he was gone, leaving me standing there with my tongue metaphorically hanging out. Well, maybe literally, too. I was going to dinner with him. That was fucking amazing.

A couple hours later, Carlos picked me up in Frida the Fiesta to do my weekly shopping. He'd named the beat-up, ramshackle car after his idol Frida Kahlo. A disastrous choice. Anyone who saw the Selma Hayek biopic knows that Frida Kahlo had dreadful health issues all her life. And so did Frida the Fiesta.

Seriously, it was a terrible car. The vinyl seats were ripped and the transmission only had three working gears out of five. Carlos had stripped out the other two and, as he shifted from first to third to fourth, it wasn't hard to see how he'd done it. Still, we weren't walking and we weren't going far.

I live a half a mile from Ghetto Ron's, so named because it used to be the absolute worst store in the Ron's supermarket chain in the absolute worst neighborhood. Now the neighborhood was up-and-coming and the store had been completely redone, so it was the nicest Ron's you could find. But the name stuck. It would always be Ghetto Ron's.

"Dog came over," I said, as Carlos ground his way into first and pulled away from the curb.

"Dios mio, Lynette, did you fuck him?"

"No, I kissed him."

"Well, that must have been a terrible let down."

"That's the thing, it wasn't."

"Oh no, that's not good. The lips are the window to the soul."

"No, Carlotta. The eyes are the window to the soul."

"Only for people who don't like to kiss."

"He's taking me to dinner tomorrow night."

Carlos gasped. "He wants to be your boyfriend."

"Well, I mean, I think he wants to get to know me. That doesn't necessarily mean he wants to be my boyfriend."

"He wants to talk to you. You don't have to talk to people to fuck them. Trust me, I know. Everybody wants to fuck me, but nobody wants to talk to me. He wants more from you. You wait and see."

I wasn't sure how I felt about that. Did I want more? Did I want him to want more? I was pretty sure I was just lusting. I wanted to have sex with him again, and as soon as I did I'd want him to go away. Maybe.

"So Carlotta, when did you know you were in love with Donald?" I asked. Normally, I avoided talking about Carlos' ex-boyfriend since it could cause a nasty tantrum, but I really wanted to know the answer.

"I knew I loved him the minute he put his penis into my mouth. And then...I knew I didn't love him the minute he put his penis into Roger Tyler's mouth."

The breakup with Donald had been epic, lasting longer than the relationship. "That's not what you said before. You said it wasn't the sex that bothered you, it was the lying."

"He didn't call me and tell me he was going to have sex with Roger Tyler before he did. It was a lie of commission."

As we pulled into the grocery store's parking lot, I tried not to imagine what Carlos might have been like if Donald had actually called to ask permission to fuck Roger Tyler. I doubted it would have a reasonable conversation.

We'd barely been inside the store for five minutes when Carlos said, "You really need to learn to cook.

Everything you eat is processed."

I glanced over at his cart and said, "You bought half the same things I did."

"I can cook though. I buy crappy food because I'm depressed and hate my life. It's entirely different."

"I could be depressed," I said, though I knew perfectly well I wasn't.

"No, you—wait, you could be. You're about to lose your job. That's depressing."

"Chuckie Cooper is not going to get me fired. Oh look. Canned chili is on sale." Carlos rolled his eyes. I explained, "You get shredded cheese, sour cream and corn tortillas and it's just like you've cooked."

"Without the cooking part."

"If it tastes good, I say eat it."

"Lynette, how are you ever going to get a man if you can't cook?" Carlos asked at the top of his lungs. A middle-aged woman and her elderly mother looked at the ceiling pretending we weren't there, and then suddenly turned down the household cleaners aisle.

I lowered my voice and said to Carlos, "I have plenty of other charms. I'm just not going to shout about them at the grocery store."

"Lynette, when you whisper you're still shouting. You just have that kind of personality." Carlos didn't like the look on my face. "Come on, let's go get food for Patsy and Edina."

Moments later we were in the pet food aisle loading up his cart with a thirty-pound bag of dog food for his two problematic pit bulls.

I was almost at the hospital when my cell rang. Fortunately, my truck has hands-free so I could pick up the call by just hitting a button.

"Hey Fetch, what's going on?"

"Hey Dog. I'm here with Tim."

"Hey Tim."

"Have you checked your email?" Tim asked.

"No, I'm driving to work. What's in my email?"

"Chuckie sent out a blast to the entire team," Fetch said, breathless.

"He wants us all to email Bob and tell him to fire the cocktail waiter from last night," Tim added.

"He calls him 'that flitty little waiter.'"

"You're not going to do that, are you?" I asked.

"Um, well, no..."

"It seems really mean," Tim agreed.

"We might tell Chuckie we did, though," Fetch admitted.

"Why would you do that? Just tell him no."

"Yeah, but four guys have already emailed to say they did it."

"Five," Tim corrected.

"That sucks," I said, pulling into the hospital parking lot. "That *really* sucks."

"I know, man. Where's a queeny guy like that going to get another job?" Fetch wondered.

"If he's not going to work in a gay bar—"

"I'm sure there are lots of things he could do," I said, defensively.

"Oh, so maybe we *should* email Bob?"

"And tell him to fire Lionel?"

"No!" I practically shouted. "Lionel didn't do anything wrong. Chuckie's being an asshole."

"Wait, who's Lionel?" Fetch asked.

"The faggy waiter," Tim said, exasperated.

"Oh, that's his name? Good to know."

Right away I was afraid that meant Fetch *was* going

to call Bob. I mean, he didn't need to remember Lionel's name for any other reason. "Didn't you say something like 'Snap, he got you, Chuckie?' when Lionel stuck up for himself?"

"I already sent him an apology about that."

"We were all drinking," agreed Tim. "You should never take what someone says in a bar too seriously."

"Chuckie understands."

"You shouldn't have apologized," I said. "Chuckie deserved what he got. He shouldn't have called Lionel nelly. And a flamer. And whatever else he said."

"I mean, he is though, right?" Fetch asked.

"You'd think he'd have a thicker skin. People must say things to him all the time."

"Why should they? Why is it anyone's business?"

"He kind of puts it out there."

"He's very in your face."

"But Fetch, you're a black guy. People must say stupid things to you all the time. Maybe you need a thicker skin."

"Fuck you, Dog."

"Yeah, Dog, I don't know if that's a fair analogy," Tim agreed.

I parked my truck but left it running. Turning it off would have killed the call. "Why isn't it a fair analogy?"

"I was born black."

"Yeah, he was born black."

"I don't know how people get to be butch or femme. But I don't remember making a decision to be the way I am. Do either of you?"

I did remember being relieved that I wasn't like the kids in high school who got called sissy and faggot all the time. I remember it felt good that I could play sports and pretend to be straight. Yeah, I didn't fit in, but no one knew I didn't fit in. It was safer to pretend. It's always safer to pretend. Then I realized that if the thing with Lionel and Chuckie had happened two months before, I'd probably email Bob and tell him to fire Lionel just to make Chuckie happy.

I didn't like feeling that about myself, but it also made me remember why Fetch was being the way he was being. "Look, you guys do what you've got to do. Just think about it, okay?"

"Yeah, sure."

"No hard feelings?"

"Either way?"

"It's cool," I assured them.

Turning the truck off, I went into the hospital. Of course, none of this should have come as a surprise. We all knew how Chuckie was. Last season we'd come in dead last, but there wasn't much Chuckie was willing to do about it. A couple of us had talked to Linda Sue about joining the team. She used to be a professional athlete, right? Even in a dress she'd play better ball than most of us. But when we brought the idea up to Chuckie he just about flipped.

"No straight guys," he said flatly.

"Linda Sue's not your average straight guy," Simon had pointed out.

"I don't care what he is. He's not playing with us."

"She," I said. "I think it's polite to say she."

"He's not trans, he's a transvestite. My sister is trans. I'm not giving the same respect to a straight guy who likes to raid his wife's closet."

There wasn't too much to say to that, so we let it drop.

The security guard waved me by when I showed my ID, so I didn't have to wait in line to go through the metal detector. I got into the elevator. Pressed eight. There were two other people going to lower floors. I didn't pay much attention. For some reason I started thinking about what it was like when I first started going to the bars. I didn't fit in there and, for the first time in my life, I didn't know how to pretend I fit in. I mean, I didn't know anything about Lady Gaga or *Project Runway* or the Kardashians. I actually had a guy once laugh at me because I couldn't name a single drag queen.

"Seriously? Not even Harvey Fierstein?" He'd asked. I just shrugged. Why would a drag queen be named Harvey? I thought they all had silly names?

The first couple of years that I was out, or whatever, weren't so great. Then I found the gay bowling league. That made things better. I fit in. I was a good bowler, so that helped. And some of the guys knew about sports. And then I started with the Birdmen. For the first time I really felt like I fit in.

Things were good. I liked playing with the Birdmen. I shouldn't mess with that. I probably shouldn't have told Fetch not to email Bob. I didn't really know Lionel. I mean, I liked him but big deal. I couldn't really see myself with someone like that. Not for more than a few dates. I needed to stay out of the mess with Chuckie. If the guys wanted to email Bob, well that was up to them. *I* wasn't going to email Bob. Beyond that it wasn't my business.

I walked into the room where I worked. The far wall was wall-to-wall windows looking out at the sprawl of Los Angeles County. That was nice. It gave patients something to look at. Three treadmills were spread across the wide room. Along the inside wall were cabinets where we kept supplies. Most of the drawers were empty. We didn't need that many supplies. I used one for my keys and wallet and a light jacket if it was chilly. On the south wall was a row of plastic chairs for people to wait in.

I almost didn't notice the old guy sitting there

because I was wondering if I should just not show up for dinner with Lionel. That wouldn't be very nice. He'd think I was an incredible asshole. But maybe that would be good. If he thought I was an asshole it would be over. I could change my mind and he could blame the whole thing on me. The problem was, I didn't want Lionel thinking I was an asshole.

The old guy cleared his throat. I glanced at my watch, but before I could really focus he said, "I'm early. Sorry."

"No problem."

The guy was in his sixties, his skin pale and chalky, his lips a bit blue. Heart patients were funny. They either looked just fine and the problems going on inside were a big surprise or they were like this guy. He obviously had problems. I knew from experience that his test wasn't going to go so well. Whatever result we got would lead to something. Best case, he'd have to have a relatively simple procedure like an angio. Worst case, he was in for some open-heart surgery. Either way, his stress test was a step toward making things better.

And then I remembered Lionel saying that I helped save lives. He was right. I did. I guess I needed someone to remind me of that.

CHAPTER FIVE

The rest of Monday was a complete disaster. When Carlos and I arrived at the front of the store to check out, a manager swooped down on us, pulled us aside and said, "Look, I'm sorry to have to say this, but you're very loud and very inappropriate and you've upset the other customers. If you don't learn to behave when you're in the store we'll have to ask you not to come back."

I stared at him for a moment. He wasn't much older than me. He tried to dress with authority, but his scraggly mustache and the extra weight he carried below the belt—making him look like a ripe pear—undermined any authority he mustered.

'The problem is, loud and inappropriate are two of my best qualities. I'm not sure I can do without them."

Carlos' mouth fell open. "Oh no, you didn't...Lynette, just tell the man you're sorry."

"*I'm* sorry? You're the one who was talking about your ex-boyfriend's penis."

"We were still in the car when I said that."

"Were we? Really? Shit."

"Out. Both of you. Now," the manager said.

We had to walk away from our groceries. As we did, I

noticed the woman with her elderly mother checking out at the end of the line of registers. She had to be the one who'd reported us to the manager, since there was barely anyone else in the store. Which was ridiculous since we'd hardly done anything. Except be obviously gay.

When we got outside, Carlos said, "I can't believe you got us thrown out of Ron's."

I decided not to argue about which of us was more responsible. Obviously, it was Carlos, but I didn't want to make him feel bad.

"I should have said something about your outfit before we left," he continued.

"What's wrong with my outfit?"

"Those heels with those shorts? Really, Lynette."

"These are boy shoes."

I was wearing a pair of three-inch platform saddle shoes from the late seventies that I'd found at Out of the Closet. They were ah-mazing. I paired them with tube socks—new but still very period—denim shorts and a pink Hello Kitty tee that almost covered my belly button. The shirt wasn't exactly my size.

"Still," Carlos said. "You look like Jodie Foster in *Taxi Driver*."

"Are you trying to say I'm butch?"

"I'm trying to say the way you dress got us thrown out of Ron's."

We climbed back into Frida the Fiesta and Carlos asked, "Where do you want to go?"

"TJ's? Albert's?" Both were likely to be more expensive but we didn't have a lot of options.

"Can we get that far?"

"Maybe."

Then it took ten minutes to get Frida started, and that only happened when I got out and pushed her across the parking lot so Carlos could pop the clutch.

After that he was afraid to turn her off, so we went to the 7-Eleven and took turns going in and grabbing the barest of necessities, while Frida coughed and sputtered in the parking lot.

So, that was why on Tuesday when I was showering for my dinner date with Dog I had no shampoo and had to wash my hair with hand soap. Which meant my hair was clean but not soft or silky. It was coarse and uncomfortable. A terrible way to go on a date. And a first date, too.

Fucking never counts as an actual date, by the way.

And then, to make matters worse, I cut myself shaving. I had this nice, leaking, half-inch cut on my Adam's apple. I spent a good ten minutes trying to staunch the flow of blood before I gave up and slathered my neck in aftershave. I let out a bloodcurdling scream as the alcohol in the aftershave closed the cut and was relieved that my neighbors were too indolent (or possibly drugged) to call the police.

Of course, none of this was as problematic as deciding what to wear. Carlos had drawn my wardrobe choices into question and I really did want things to go well with Dog, so I decided to tone it down a little. Well, okay, a lot. I was absolutely sure I could do toned-down and subtle. No problem.

So, I started with a pair of jeans. Jeans are simple, easy, they don't draw much attention, everyone wears them. I even had a pair that didn't have any slits near the crotch or fancy stitching or rhinestones on the back pocket. So, I had one toned-down, subtle item of clothing all picked out. And it wouldn't matter at all if I wore my fluorescent pink boxer briefs underneath.

Since it was dinner, I thought maybe I should get a little dressed up and I happened to have the perfect sports jacket. It was a velvet aubergine that looked black in most lights. A lot of people think aubergine and eggplant are the same color. They're not. They're completely different. My bedroom walls were eggplant; my jacket was aubergine. The best way to understand the difference is to imagine that you're holding an actual eggplant under a light. The part of the vegetable that attracts light, that's eggplant; while the part that doesn't attract light and is almost black, that's aubergine. Subtle, right?

With the jeans and aubergine sports jacket I decided to wear a simple, pink oxford shirt. Such a pale pink it was almost white. I had an old pair of black penny loafers that I decided to wear without socks. I don't know why, but wearing shoes without socks always seems classier, as though you're saying to the world, 'Of course, I can afford socks, but I simply can't be bothered. I'm too busy yachting and drinking champagne to spend time buying silly socks.'

Assembled, the outfit was classy—a practically black jacket with a practically white shirt, how much more toned down can you get? But it lacked something. That's when I remembered the yellow Hermes scarf my grandmother had left to my mother and I had borrowed out of her things when I left home. My father would have said stolen, but really I know she would have left it to me if she'd known she was going to die—and if she'd known I was the sort of boy who could rock an Hermes scarf. Anyway, I folded it carefully and put it into my breast pocket, letting it just peek out. There, I was done.

I went into my living room and sat down to wait for Dog.

I sat in my truck wondering what to do. I was there,

so obviously I was going on the date. But, should I tell Lionel about Chuckie's email to the team? Just because Chuckie was trying to get Lionel fired didn't mean it would work. Bob wasn't a bad guy. He'd gotten drunk with the team one time and he actually seemed like a good guy. Maybe he'd just give Lionel a different shift. The team came in on Sundays, so maybe Lionel could have Sundays off. Of course, I was pretty sure Chuckie was a regular every day after work. Usually, I went to The Bird only on Sundays, but any other time I stopped in Chuckie was there. So, maybe changing Lionel's shift wouldn't work.

Well. Bob might not do anything. He could always tell the team no and not fire Lionel. Maybe this would all work out and nothing would happen. Which meant I shouldn't tell Lionel. It would hurt his feelings. Not that he'd show it. I'd already figured out that much about him. He'd act like it didn't matter, but I couldn't see how it wouldn't. It would matter to me.

I got out of the truck and walked up to his apartment, wondering on the way if he'd called the landlord yet about the broken security gate. When he answered the door he wore a very purple jacket, a pink shirt and a crazy yellow scarf flopping out of his pocket. I had to blink my eyes a couple times.

"Wow, you dressed up," I said, thinking I was lucky he wasn't wearing red plaid pants.

"No, honey, you should see me when I dress up."

"Oh, well, you look nice." Mostly I said it so he wouldn't go change. I'd been planning to take him to a Mexican place, but as soon as I saw him changed my mind. I knew a lot of guys who went there. I tried to think of a place we could go where we'd never run into anyone I knew. I drew a blank for a minute and then I remembered this old-timey restaurant my parents went to once a year for their anniversary. Massie's.

"You look...nice, too." He wasn't being any more truthful than I was. I guess it's true that I looked a lot more casual. I had my brown California T-shirt on—the one with the state animal drawn on it, a grizzly bear—jeans and an old pair of Vans. It was also true that I really didn't get much more dressed up than that. I had a dark suit somewhere for job interviews and funerals, and since this wasn't either of those I hadn't bothered to find it.

"I guess, we should go," I said. Then we walked out to my truck.

I love my truck. It's a six month-old Ford F-150, gray, sports package with custom rims I had put on that make it a good six inches further off the ground than standard. I hit my fob to unlock the passenger door and hurried ahead to open it for Lionel.

"Oh my, a gentleman."

Using the step bar he climbed up into the cab. I walked around and got in, made myself comfortable behind the wheel.

"Everything's so clean. Is it brand new?" he asked, as I pushed the button to start the truck.

"I've had it for about six months."

"It looks like you've never used it."

"I like to take care of my things." That wasn't exactly true. I liked to take care of my truck, though sooner or later I'd give up and it would get filled with take-out containers and receipts and handwritten directions, just like the six year-old Explorer I traded in.

Lionel glanced at my T-shirt, which was a bit worn but didn't say anything. The shirt was clean, though. I think that counts.

"Where are we going?" he asked.

"Massie's, downtown." Downtown was only three-quarters of a mile. Just far enough not to walk.

"Oh my. That is nice. If I'd known, I really would have dressed up." I gave him a panicked glance and he smiled at me. "Of course, it's California. Everyone's so casual. I could wear a tiara and flip-flops and no one would bat an eye."

I didn't think that was entirely true. "The flip-flops wouldn't get you much attention."

"No, you're right. People would have a conniption over the tiara. Isn't that weird though? You can run around practically naked and nobody cares, but you put some rhinestones on your head and they freak out."

I didn't know what to say to that, so I acted like the road needed my attention. It didn't, there were only a few more blocks to the restaurant and practically no traffic. Lionel mumbled something beside me.

"What?"

"I always like to find new places to wear diamonds."

"Okay."

"It's something Marilyn Monroe says in *Gentlemen Prefer Blondes*. She'd just discovered what a tiara is."

"How could she not know what a tiara was?"

"This was before TV. People barely knew anything before TV. Cultural illiteracy was rampant."

I turned onto Cedar and almost immediately pulled into the parking garage next to Massie's. I took the parking ticket from the machine, hoping the restaurant validated. I found a spot near the elevator, then we got out and I hit the fob to lock my truck. We weren't saying much. I was nervous, and when Lionel did say things, a little lost. I wondered if he was nervous, too. I didn't think he would be. It seemed out of character. But still...

"I haven't been here since my parents brought me for my high school graduation," I said.

"I got a GED so we skipped the whole family dinner thing. Or we would have if we were speaking."

"I'm sorry. Maybe I shouldn't talk about my family."

"Oh Gawd, don't edit yourself. You have a happy family. That's nice."

I didn't remind him that I wasn't out to my mom and dad. Once in a while I'd wonder how things would go if I did come out to them. That would give me nightmares for a week.

Massie's is a storefront off the lobby of a fifteen-story building built in 1928. I know that because there's a plaque as you come in the revolving door. It's some kind of historical landmark and the architect was famous—or at least, locally famous. The restaurant itself feels very open with plate glass windows looking into the lobby and also out to the street on two other sides. The only wall without windows had doors to the kitchen and a tiny bar.

The host led us to a small table next to the window looking out at Ocean Boulevard. Before we'd had a chance to open the menus, our waiter was there.

"Hi, my name is Trevin and I'll be your waiter this evening." Trevin was in his mid-forties with dyed hair and puffy pink skin. He was immediately too friendly. "How about I get you two something from the bar?"

"What kind of beer do you have?" I asked.

"Okay," Trevin said. "We have forty-eight kinds of beer. So in the interest of getting you a drink sometime this evening, let's narrow it down. Domestic, foreign or artisan?"

"Domestic."

Trevin squinted at me. "Sam Adams."

"Um, okay."

Trevin looked at Lionel, asking, "And what would you like? I have the feeling it's going to be interesting."

"Sapphire martini, straight up, four olives, whisper vermouth but not very close to the glass."

"A man after my own heart," Trevin said with a smile. Then he walked away.

"Do you know him?" I asked.

"Never saw him before in my life."

"He's awfully friendly."

"He can tell we're on a date."

"Oh, okay." I worried that everyone in the restaurant could tell we were on a date. I mean, I knew I should be okay with things like that, but I wasn't really. I didn't like people knowing my business. I mean, I didn't know things about them, why did they get to know things about me?

Lionel looked over the menu while I looked over the restaurant. It was nearly full. A lot of the people there were middle-aged or older. Most were more dressed up than Lionel. There were a couple of families, a lot of couples, and a few tables with just two guys. The couples were probably on dates, and so were the guys. If I could figure out what they were doing, then they could figure out—

I stuck my nose into the menu. Don't think about what other people are thinking, I told myself. Think about what to have for dinner. They looked like they had a nice New York Steak. They had chicken in a puff pastry that could be good. And salmon. A nice piece of salmon in beurre blanc might be best.

Lionel was still reading his menu so I took a good look at him. His jaw was square and there was a light brown bristle on his chin and cheeks—like no matter how often he shaved he still needed to shave. His hair was highlighted with blond streaks. I guessed somewhere underneath it was dishwater blond. His cheeks were high and his eyes were a piercing dark blue. It took me a moment to realize he was staring at me.

"See something you like?"

I blushed and he chuckled. *Screw it*, I thought. "Yeah, I do see something I like. Something I like a lot."

Crap. I was being stupid, worrying about the other people in the restaurant. Worrying about what they thought. I'd been out in public with guys before. Lots of times. I'd just never been out in public with someone like Lionel, someone so obviously gay. But even that shouldn't be a problem. I didn't think there was anything wrong with being gay. I really didn't. So, if Lionel was obviously gay, that shouldn't be a big deal.

No, *I* didn't think there was anything wrong with being gay, but I was all too aware that other people did. Lots of other people.

CHAPTER SIX

I was absolutely terrified we were going Dutch. I mean, Dog had made a point of saying he was "taking" me to dinner. Usually that would mean he'd be paying. Of course, for some people it might just mean they were going to drive. I didn't know Dog well enough to be a hundred percent sure which he meant. Unfortunately, I'd barely brought enough cash for my half—I'd been expecting someplace cheaper—and even that was cash I'd set aside for my rent.

I probably shouldn't have ordered a martini. Worse! I ordered top shelf gin. There weren't any prices on the menu for a mixed drink, so I had to guess how much it would be. My guess was about twelve dollars. Obviously, I could only have one. Not that I *should* have more than one martini on a date, but I at least liked to have the option.

Trevin floated back with our drinks. He set a frosted mug in front of Dog and poured beer into it. I reminded myself I needed to get Dog's last name and phone number before the evening was finished. I couldn't go on forever calling him just Dog. I really should know if it's Dog Smith or Dog Jones. You're never truly intimate with a person until you know their last name.

"Would you boys like to order?"

I would have been fine just enjoying our drinks for a few minutes, but Dog jumped on the opportunity to order.

"What do you want?" he asked.

I ordered a twenty-five dollar piece of chicken. It came with a truffle cream sauce. I knew that truffles were a sort of mushroom, so basically a twenty-five dollar chicken breast with cream of mushroom soup on it. Between the entrée, the drink, tax and tip, I'd have been able to eat all week on what I, he, someone, was spending on me. Well, almost a week.

Dog ordered salmon in a fancy sauce then handed his menu to the waiter. I gave mine up as well. Trevin smiled and walked away. I took a sip of my martini. It was perfect.

Oh Gawd, I thought, *I have to think up something to say*.

I was not fond of dating. In fact, I hadn't done much of it. I'd had entire relationships that hadn't included anything remotely like a date. In fact, I probably would have been more comfortable with Dog if he'd just wanted to fuck again. If he'd asked nicely once or twice, I probably would have given in. But, no, he wanted to talk to me. That seemed kind of perverted.

"So tell me about losing your virginity?" I asked. It seemed like a good date question. Not that I had time to write Miss Manners and ask.

"Boy or girl?"

"Oh Gawd! Boy! I hope you've blocked sex with a girl from your mind. Memories like that can be so scarring."

"It wasn't *that* bad," he said.

"Obviously, it wasn't that good either."

"No, I guess not."

I couldn't help smiling at him. He was fun to tease. I hoped he didn't mind being teased. "So, boy. Tell me."

"I played football in high school. Linebacker. At an away game we stayed in a hotel, I shared a room with the center."

"Football is a foreign language to me. Get to the sex."

He blushed a bit. I like a man with good circulation.

"Um, well, we shared a room and in the middle of the night he crawled into my bed. The next day he acted like he hated my guts. It was weird."

"Hmmmm...first of all, I've seen that in a porno. Second of all, you represented his forbidden desires," I said, somewhat dramatically. "You had to be destroyed."

"He didn't actually—"

"Metaphorically. I bet he's married with at least two children by now."

"Three. The first one was senior year."

"She's got something to prove."

"She? No, I was talking about—"

"I mean she in the queer he's-a-she kind of way."

"Oh, yeah. I've heard people do that." He frowned suggesting it wasn't something he agreed with. "So, what about you? When did you..."

"Tenth grade. My English teacher."

"You—that's not, it's not legal."

"Oh, did you mean the first time I had legal sex?"

"No, I just, um, wow...I'm sorry about that."

I'd gotten this reaction before. I did not enjoy it. "I was sixteen. And I seduced him."

"Yeah, but—"

"Look, I understand the whole consent thing. And the whole violation of trust thing. But I wanted it and I enjoyed it. I don't like people deciding that I'm a victim.

I told this one guy I was seeing and he was like, 'Holy shit! You were raped.' I was not raped. The age of consent in most states is actually sixteen. If I'd had sex with my English teacher in Nevada, it would have been completely legal. Just because it was illegal in California doesn't mean I was traumatized." I realized I was getting sort of passionate about the whole thing. "Sorry...soapbox."

He glanced around uncomfortably to see if people were looking at us. I guess they were. Still, he was nice enough to say, "It's okay. It happened to you. You get to decide how to feel about it."

"Thank you." We were quiet. Sipped our drinks. *I should probably stop telling that story*, I thought. It didn't make for good first date conversation.

"So, boyfriends?" I asked, plunging onward.

"One. It lasted almost a year."

I was tempted to ask what happened, but ex boyfriends were terrible first date topics, as well. Of course, then we'd be even. But there was no guarantee he'd even had a terrible breakup, so maybe we wouldn't be even.

Before I could move on he asked, "And you? Boyfriends?"

"Depends on how we define boyfriend. A month, too many to count. Six months, zero. But, I'm only twenty-three. I'm still sowing my wild oats." Oh Gawd, I'd just made myself sound like a committed slut. I scrambled to think of something to say that was a little bit more relationship-y. "It might be time to harvest my oats and make oatmeal."

"Oh, okay," he said. He had a frightened look on his face. And who can blame him? He asked about boyfriends and I talked about oatmeal. Gawd, he probably thinks I'm a freak.

Trevin brought out our dinners on an excessively large tray, set them on a stand and laid them in front of us with a bit of flare. Then he asked if we might like a glass of wine with dinner. We both shook our heads. It was tempting, but not only could I not afford a ten-dollar glass of wine, I'd already said plenty of stupid things. Alcohol only made my tendency for stupidity worse.

Dog looked like he might be sick. I wondered if he'd changed his mind about the fish.

"Excuse me," he said, getting up and walking—not to the men's room, which looked to be on the side of the restaurant with the kitchen—no, he walked out of the restaurant entirely. Into the building's lobby and then out onto the street. I watched as he walked toward the parking garage where we'd left his truck.

His face turned away, as though he didn't want to risk looking at me.

Lionel was saying something about oatmeal that didn't make a lot of sense, when I looked over and saw the host seating my parents on the other side of Massie's. I wanted to throw up. They couldn't see me there with Lionel. I mean, I could have lied about who Lionel was, but I couldn't think of a believable lie. I couldn't say he was a friend; they'd grill me on why I even had a friend like Lionel. I couldn't say he was someone I worked with; I didn't have the sort of job where I needed to socialize with my fellow workers. I could say he was on the softball team; but they didn't even know about the *gay* softball team. There was just no logical reason I would be with someone like Lionel...except the truth.

And they couldn't find out the truth. It would kill my dad. So I got up, turned my face away from my parents and walked out of the restaurant.

When I got to my truck, I decided to call Lionel and try to explain. Except we'd never traded numbers. And I didn't know his last name. None of my friends knew his full name either. They just called him the queeny waiter at The Bird, or the faggy waiter, or the girly waiter. I doubted directory assistance would be able to look him up under any of those names. I could call The Bird and ask, or I could go to his apartment and see if his last name was on the mailbox.

Except, he was going to hate me no matter what.

Crap. Abandoning him in the middle of dinner. What a shitty thing to do. What would I even say to him if I did have his phone number? I mean, when I told him I wasn't out to my parents he hadn't been exactly understanding. He'd made that joke about CPR. Like it would be okay to give my dad a heart attack because I could save him. It was never good to have a heart attack, and even though I knew CPR there wasn't any guarantee I could save my dad. And what did Lionel think I was going to do, go over to my parents house with a defibrillator and say, 'Hi, Dad, there's something I have to tell you. Let me plug this in first." No, the thing with Lionel was over. There wasn't anything I could do about that. At least not at that particular moment. And probably never. Yeah, definitely never.

I started my truck and drove out of the garage.

And what were my parents doing at Massie's? Their anniversary was a long time ago and they weren't the kind of people who'd treat themselves to a nice dinner just because. Something must have happened. Something good.

I pressed the phone button on my steering wheel and told the system to "CALL MADISON." I hated talking to my dashboard, but it did make more sense than scrolling through my contacts one by one. The phone rang a couple of times and my sister picked up.

"Hey, how's it going?"

"Not bad. The kids are going to bed in about twenty minutes. You want to call me back then?"

"Oh that's okay. I just have a quick question. Is something going on with mom and dad?"

"What do you mean?"

"They're having dinner at Massie's. Are they celebrating something?"

"Mom got accepted at Cal State to do her master's." My mom was an RN at Memorial. Had been since I was a kid. She'd gotten me my first hospital job as an orderly when I was eighteen. I kind of remembered her telling me she was thinking of going back for her master's. Which was great. For her.

"She didn't tell you?" Maddy asked.

"Maybe."

"Men. You never remember anything. I bet you don't remember giving them a gift card to Massie's either."

"Wait? They hadn't used that yet?" I'd given them dinner at Massie's for their last anniversary. Eight, nine months before.

"It was about to expire."

That meant they were at Massie's because of me. Without even trying I'd sabotaged my own date. Great.

"What were you doing at Massie's?"

"Oh, I wasn't there. I mean, I was driving by and saw them going in."

"Oh. Okay. So, you're not going to call me back in twenty minutes."

"That was all I needed. I mean, we can hang out on the weekend, if you want."

"No. You're having dinner with us tomorrow.

Remember? I have a surprise for you."

Another fix-up. That's why I'd forgotten it. I was trying to.

"Maddy, I told you no more blind dates."

"It's not a date. How can it be a date with Arthur and I staring at the two of you?"

"You know I don't like being fixed up." We'd been round and round about this. Unfortunately, I kept losing and having to spend the occasional evening making small talk with Maddy's co-workers, friends, and friends of friends.

"I've already promised," she said. "Tomorrow night. Seven o'clock."

And then she hung up.

Of course, I could just tell Maddy I was gay. *She* wasn't going to have a heart attack. But I was afraid she'd tell Mom, and if they both knew, it was only a matter of time until one of them slipped and told my dad.

I was home. I parked the truck in my space and just sat for a bit. My ex-boyfriend Daniel crossed my mind. The fact that I wasn't out to my family had been a huge deal for him. He wanted to meet them and go for holidays and do all the things we did with his family. And we did tons of things with his family, weekends in Palm Springs, Dodgers games, monthly potlucks.

So, Daniel, and his whole extended family, had a lot of trouble understanding why I wasn't out to my family. He started a lot of sentences with, "In this day and age..." and, "This isn't the nineteen-seventies..." It took a toll on the relationship and we finally called it quits.

Not that I thought Lionel would be any more comfortable with my not being out to my family. Or out at work. No, he didn't seem like the kind of guy who would put up with that. So, it was probably just as well that I'd screwed things up. I was bound to do it eventually.

Crap. I felt horrible about leaving him that way, though. That's when I realized there was something I could do that would make it at least a little bit better.

CHAPTER SEVEN

I had absolutely no fucking idea what I was going to do. Dog had just gotten up and left. Vanished. At first, I wondered if maybe he'd left something important in his truck. Like he forgot some medication he needed to take with food. That would explain the nauseated look on his face. But when he didn't come back after ten minutes. I said, "Fuck it," and ate my dinner. It was a little chilled but still tasty. Not twenty-five dollars worth of tasty, but tasty.

Oh my Gawd. How would I get out of there? I had nowhere near enough money in my pocket to cover the entire dinner. And I didn't have a credit card. I'd screwed up pretty badly with that kind of thing when I was nineteen, and twenty, and twenty-one, so my life was now on a strictly cash basis. I didn't even have a debit card. This was going to be horrible. Really horrible.

I could call Carlos, but he didn't have any money either. And even if he did have enough cash lying around, I'd have to pay him back immediately. Which meant I'd be short for my rent. And that was going to be a problem. The only way to pay it on time would be to open my CD, which meant I'd make absolutely no money on my tiny investment—and I'd probably end up spending more than just what I needed and never get a car—so I hated that idea.

Of course, I did know guys with money who'd give me a loan. Some I'd dated, some I hadn't. Yet. But no matter. If I called any of them, they'd expect a little something for bailing me out. And I wasn't in the mood for that. Something about telling Dog that I was ready for oatmeal made sowing more oats—even at a small profit— less appealing.

But that was ridiculous. What kind of person would walk out of a restaurant in the middle of a date? It felt shitty. Not so much because he'd done it to me. I knew there were assholes in the world. That lesson had been driven home a few times. No, the part that felt so shitty was that I hadn't thought he was one of them. I thought he was a good guy. And I was wrong.

Trevin came over to the table and asked if I was finished.

"I am, thank you." I wanted to think of a way to stall but I'd cleaned the plate so well it really didn't even need to go through the dishwasher.

"Is your friend coming back?" he asked, far too sympathetically.

"I'm sure he is. He had to go to his truck to get something. Something important."

"Should I take his dinner back and keep it warm?"

"Um. Not yet. He might be a little bit longer." Or he might never come back.

"Well, would you like another martini while you wait?"

It was tempting but it wasn't a good idea to make matters worse. When I said no Trevin offered me cappuccino.

"How about regular coffee?" I asked. That would

only add three bucks to the check. Three bucks was not the end of the world. Plus I needed to stall. I needed time to think of something. Anything.

When Trevin walked away I started to do math in my head. This was rarely a good idea but I had no choice. Our drinks came to about twenty dollars. The two entrées were around sixty. That added up to eighty. Plus the three or four dollars for my coffee. And, of course, a generous tip. That put me at roughly a hundred dollars. I had fifty-six in my pocket. So, I had to find someone to borrow fifty dollars from. I'd be a hundred dollars short for my rent, but I could deal with that problem later.

Of course, the whole situation wasn't improved by the fact that I may or may not even have a job. No, I had a job. It was Tuesday, after all. Chuckie Cooper had had two days to get me fired. *If* he were going to do it, it would have happened already. Plus Bob liked me. He wasn't going to fire me. No matter how important Chuckie Cooper thought he was. Everything was going to be fine. I just needed to beg someone for a shift or two in order to make my rent. I might be able to pick something up in the dining room. Hell, I'd bus tables if they'd let me.

Still, I didn't get on the phone to call around for the money I needed. I decided to give Dog a few more minutes to come back. With a really good explanation. A really amazing explanation. Like the most amazing explanation anyone had ever given to anything.

Suddenly, I had the eerie feeling I'd seen this movie before. My life had turned into some kind of cable channel thriller about a woman whose date vanishes and then when she tries to find him no one remembers seeing him. Like he never existed. Is she crazy? Or is she trapped in the middle of a conspiracy?

Trevin was back with my coffee. He set it down in

front of me. Next to the coffee he set down a square plate with a creamer and bowl of sugar.

"First date?" he asked. Okay, so Trevin remembered Dog. Which meant I wasn't in a thriller. No, I was in some stupid sitcom where the main character is constantly humiliated.

"Yeah. First and last."

"I have to say, I have seen this happen before. Though I've never seen it happen to anyone as cute as you."

"Oh, thanks," I said, smiling weakly. Being a waiter myself, I knew not to trust the flirtation. In all likelihood he was working me for a better tip. That's what I would do. I mean, it's almost rude not to flirt with customers.

Trevin winked and walked away.

Sipping my coffee, I tried to think what would make a good excuse for Dog's disappearance. Looking on the bright side, he might have gotten really sick. Too sick to actually say he was sick. Hell, he could be sitting in his truck, dead. I was almost certain I could forgive him if he died. I tried to think of other situations I would find forgivable. I supposed if aliens had shone an invisible tractor beam on him and pulled him out of the restaurant as a prelude to abducting him, that would be forgivable. What else? Early onset dementia; if he suddenly forgot who I was, or better yet, who he was. Well, that would be forgivable, too. Other than those three not-very-possible possibilities I didn't think there was any good reason to do what he'd done.

I decided it was time to bite the bullet and call Carlos to see if there was any remote possibility he could bring me fifty dollars and then drive me home so I could replace his fifty with fifty from the Häagen-Dazs container in my freezer that was not a Häagen-Dazs container but was actually my checking account.

Oh Gawd, I thought, *What a disaster!*

Just then Trevin came over and leaned over discretely. "Your friend just called. He paid the check over the phone."

"Did he? So he's definitely not coming back?" I'd already figured that out, but pretending surprise was not a bad idea.

"Apparently not."

"Could you box that up?" I asked, pointing at Dog's dinner. There was no reason to let good food go to waste. "And then, could you bring me everything on the dessert menu?"

"Everything?"

"You still have his credit card number, don't you?"

"Yes, I do. How about an aperitif?"

"How about two?"

###

My sister, her husband, Arthur, and their two toddlers live in a three-bedroom ranch in Bellflower about a twenty-minute drive from my apartment. I arrived the next night ten minutes early for dinner. I was not looking forward to the evening and was already dreaming up excuses to leave early. Headache, stomachache, mild fever. It probably wouldn't work, since our mom was a nurse and she had her own two kids, Maddy was very suspicious of convenient illnesses.

Unfortunately, Arthur answered the door and I hadn't had time to settle on a really good escape strategy. "Hey Dougie, come on in."

I stepped into the house and we did the straight guy pat/punch each other in the shoulder thing. He was a pretty good guy. I'd always liked him. My sister, though, had mixed feelings. She often complained that he was too safe, too boring, too ordinary. I don't know how she had time to think about these things. Two kids under five, a house and a husband. And she longed for excitement. I think I'd long for sleep.

Their place looked the way places looked when people had kids: clean but chaotic. Nothing stayed where it was supposed to for long. The living room was still baby-proofed, so there were plastic corners on the coffee tables, special latches on the entertainment center drawers, and interlocking plastic dividers to turn large chunks of the living room into an impromptu play pen, since actual playpens were out of fashion.

My two-and-a-half-year-old nephew Leland held up one of his books and said, "Truck." The book was clearly about trucks. His four-year-old sister, Leanne, was sitting on the couch, dressed entirely in pink watching some kids' show with talking ponies.

"There you are," Maddy said. "Come into the kitchen. Jen's here already.

Jen? Jen who? My stomach rumbled. I would have preferred to read Leland's book about trucks to him and then watch a story about talking ponies with Leanne. But it was not to be. I walked into the large eat-in kitchen and my jaw dropped.

Standing there was my ex-fiancée, Jennifer Berri, who I hadn't seen in probably six years and yet she somehow managed to look just the same. Tall, thin, freckled and blond.

"Hey Dougie, it's good to see you." She stepped over and kissed me on the cheek. Then in a low voice said, "Sorry about this. Maddy didn't tell me you'd be here."

"It's nice to see you." It was awful to see her. When I broke off the engagement I'd told her I was gay. She hadn't believed me.

"I ran into Jen at Whole Foods. I thought it would be nice if we all caught up."

I glared at her. She was violating the unwritten rule, that if you break up with someone your family breaks up with them, too.

"Can I get you a beer, Dougie?" Maddy asked.

"Sure."

I turned to see that Arthur hadn't followed me into the kitchen. Instead, he was on the floor reading to his son. Lucky man.

"So, how have you been?" Jennifer asked.

"Great."

"Maddy says you're some kind of medical tech at Harbor?"

"Yeah."

Handing me a PBR, Maddy was back saying, "Jen's a pharmaceutical rep now." Jennifer was the type they liked to hire. She'd look great in a business suit. "Her territory is the South Bay,"

I had a horrible feeling I knew where this was going.

"She was telling me about an interesting lunch she had a few months back. A doctor named Keller. Daniel Keller." Yup, that was the place I thought this was going. My exes had met. They've had lunch. Crap.

Jennifer made a face. "I'm so sorry. I assumed, I mean, I always knew you and Maddy were close—" She tried to smile. "It was a relief, actually. When we broke up you said... but I didn't believe you. I never believed you. Until I met Daniel."

"Can we talk?" Maddy asked, nodding her head toward the door that led to the attached garage.

"We're talking."

"In private." She grabbed my arm and dragged me out of the kitchen. As I passed her Jennifer mouthed the words, "I'm sorry."

Maddy closed the door to the main house and stared me down. I backed up against one of Maddy and Arthur's matching minivans.

"You're gay?"

"Yes." Okay, that felt better than I thought it would. In fact, it felt pretty good. Maybe this wasn't going to be so—

She punched me in the shoulder. "How can you be gay? You played football in high school."

"Lots of gay guys like sports."

"Oh I know they say things like that, I just never thought they were true. You're really gay?"

"Yes. I'm really gay."

"Why didn't you tell me? I'm okay with gay people. Did you think I'd be weird about it?" She *was* being weird about it.

"I didn't tell you because you'll tell Mom and then she'll slip up and tell Dad."

"You can't tell Dad."

"I know that."

"You used to date girls. Dad isn't going to live forever. Can't you just fudge it?"

"Do you fudge it with Arthur?"

"All the time." Then she looked at me closely and said, "Oh my God, are you one of the ones who likes to wear leather?"

"No, I like T-shirts, beer and softball."

"That's good. I'd hate to think about you having all that kinky sex."

"I don't know that it's all that—"

"Please, I'm married to Mr. Missionary-Position. Almost anything is kinky by comparison. I don't want to think about you having all that kinky sex because I'll be jealous as shit."

"Okay, I didn't need to know that."

She crossed her arms and asked, "What are we going to do?"

"Nothing. We're just going to go on like no one knows. Except, you'll stop fixing me up with girls. Okay?"

"I hope you don't expect me to fix you up with guys."

"Please don't." I had the feeling that would be every bit as mortifying as when she fixed me up with girls.

"I don't meet many gay guys driving the kids to preschool. Actually, I don't meet many adults. How am I *not* going to tell Mom? She's the only adult I talk to."

"You have Arthur to talk to."

"Like I said, Mom is the only adult I talk to."

I shrugged. "Can you think of a reason to have your jaw wired shut?"

She punched me in the shoulder again.

"Don't joke about this. Asshole."

I was serious.

CHAPTER EIGHT

On Thursday, when I arrived at The Bird for my shift, I was unceremoniously fired. Let go. Laid off. Canned.

When I walked in, Carlos was leaning against the bar, chatting intently with a tall guy in waiter's garb. Carlos turned and saw me and went white as a sheet. Not an easy feat for a brown boy. He wasn't even supposed to be there. It was his night off.

As I sauntered over, I had a dreadful feeling about what was happening; that terrible sense that something's happening and there's nothing you can do about it except let it happen. I said "Hel-lo," to Carlos, tossing in a few extra syllables to give me courage. "What's going on?"

"This is Andrew. I'm training him." I glanced at Andrew, who was so good-looking it was startling. He could have been on a magazine cover. Any magazine. Seriously, *Horse & Hound* would put him on the cover. We'd had his type before. They never seemed to worry about actually serving anyone, they just floated near the tables and collected large tips. I ignored him.

"Why are *you* here, though?" I asked Carlos.

"I have to train Andrew."

"But I could train Andrew."

Carlos looked stricken. "There's an envelope for you in the office. On the desk."

"What's in the envelope?"

"I would never open someone else's mail." He feigned insult.

"Especially when you already know what's inside."

"It's a termination letter and a severance check."

"Bob's not even going to fire me in person?"

"His lawyer advised against it."

Lance, the bartender, plunked a shot glass onto the bar and filled it with Fireball. "This one's on the house," he said, and walked away.

I threw the shot back, defiantly raised my chin, and said, "Excuse me." Then I marched back to the office. Office was a polite word for it. It was really a closet with a desk squeezed into it. On the desk, amidst the clutter of receipts and timesheets, lay an envelope with my name on it. I picked it up and opened it.

Inside, was a letter that, in the blandest, most non-committal way possible, said that I no longer had a job. In addition, there was a severance check for six weeks pay. Of course, I only made minimum wage so it wasn't enormous. Bob must have realized that because there were also three crisp one hundred dollar bills in the envelope. That gave me enough to get by for almost a month without dipping into my car money. Maybe six weeks. I had to get another job and I had to get it fast.

While it wasn't a lot of money, it did seem a lot of money to spend to keep one customer happy. I knew Chuckie Cooper was in The Bird a lot. But even if he spent a hundred dollars a week, it was going to take a long time for Bob to recoup his money—the profit on every dollar spent in a restaurant being notoriously slim.

I went back out to the bar, put one of the hundred dollar bills in front of me and ordered a Sapphire Martini from Lance. He set the martini down in front of me and pushed the crisp hundred back across the bar.

"Your money will be good tomorrow. And not one minute before."

"Thank you. You sir, are a gentleman."

"Don't mention it, darlin'."

Lance was sweet. He was nearing forty, a casual body builder and covered with tattoos from the tips of his toes up to his chin. He'd slept with just about everyone and managed to remain liked by the majority of his conquests. I had never had sex with him, but then I'm a natural born contrarian.

It was still early; there were only two customers in the bar: regulars Bill and Phil, who seemed riveted by my drama. They raised their glasses to me and made sad faces. Andrew floated around looking sullen and bored; I doubted he was either. My guess was he'd spent enough time in front of a mirror to know that pouty was his best look.

Carlos slipped onto the stool next to me. "Can you believe it?" he asked. "He's straight. Keeps talking about his girlfriend."

I shrugged. "I suppose you have to hire them. It would be discrimination not to. But really, shouldn't they stick to their own kind?"

"I know, right? But the thing is, Bob went out and found him. He was working at a place that sells sneakers. Bob went up to him and offered him a job. He's never even worked in a restaurant before."

"He recruited a straight guy?"

"He says a straight boy will create less drama."

Was that it? I'd been too much drama? But I'd only had sex with a handful of the customers, and only had a couple of cat fights with Carlos, and never gave attitude—well, seldom gave attitude—all right, always gave attitude to everyone in the bar. But, seriously, what was a bar without drama?

I looked across the bar. Andrew's pout had deepened while he played at wiping down a table, somehow making him even more attractive. "The customers will spend a fortune buying drinks while they try to seduce him."

"Exactly."

Something dreadful occurred to me. I'd have been more likely to keep my job in a gay bar if I'd been in the closet. If I'd pretended to be straight, I'd probably still be working there. That was so upside down. And depressing. I was trying really hard not to freak about the disaster my life was becoming. *Where would I get a job?* I wondered. I didn't have a car so I couldn't go too far. I could take the bus I suppose, but not without a concealed weapon.

I was nearly finished with my martini when Larry Lamour came in and ordered me another. Then he sat down, dressed like your average retiree on his way to play golf—which in his case looked so very, very wrong. He said, "I heard what happened to you. That awful man calling you names and then Bob fires you. Shameful."

"You don't have to worry about me, I've climbed out of the gutter more than once. I can do it again."

"Spoken like a true queen. People never understand how strong you have to be if you're a girly-boy."

That embarrassed me. Yes, sometimes my life was hard, but things were better than they used to be. Life had to have been much harder for Larry. I mean, he was wearing a muumuu and fruit on his head back in the days when you could get arrested for it.

"But I'm no activist. All I've ever done is wear silly hats and sing silly songs. Bill is much more the activist.

He was in a bar riot over in Wilmington years before Stonewall. Isn't that right, Bill?"

Bill hadn't heard a word Larry said, "What?"

"I SAID YOU HAVE A BIG COCK!"

Bill gave us a thumbs up.

"When I was young, I worried for awhile whether or not I was masculine enough, but then I thought, I'm gay; there isn't any way I'm going to fit into the straight world so why even try? Yes, I wear caftans; yes I wear silly hats. Who really cares?"

"People care."

"Oh I know. But none of the ones who matter to me." He sipped his drink and then said, "It amazes me that we're not all kinder. And when I say we, I don't just mean gay men, I mean the whole big we. Humanity. If you think about it, there really isn't anyone, anywhere who isn't on the outside looking in at some point in their lives; at some point everyone is the wrong color, the wrong religion, the wrong weight, the wrong age, the wrong sexuality, the wrong gender, the wrong *something*. We have so many ways of judging each other that it's hard to imagine anyone getting through life without being some kind of wrong at least some of the time."

Since I'd just lost my job I was having a little trouble caring about the whole of humanity, which must have shown on my face since Larry said, "You're not drunk enough for this kind of conversation, are you?"

I shook my head. He was right, of course. He was being sort of profound. Profound should never happen before three martinis.

"Let me get you another drink, then," he said, waving down Lance. "Give us another round, dear." Lance nodded and started our drinks. Larry continued, "I'm not surprised at Chuckie Cooper, though. I've heard plenty of stories about him. But the whole team. That does surprise me."

"The whole team?" I asked. "What do you mean?"

"It was the whole team that wanted you fired. They all sent emails to Bob."

"The team. All of them?"

"That's what I heard."

###

I was sleeping when my cell phone rang. It was still in my jeans pocket and my jeans were somewhere on the floor. I crawled off the bed and sorted through the clothes on the floor until I found my jeans. Glancing at the screen before I picked up the call I saw two things: My mom was calling and my battery was nearly dead.

"Hey," I said, accepting the call.

"Douglas?" Crap, full name. I was in trouble. "I spoke to your sister."

I left a long pause, hoping my battery would die and the conversation would be over. When it didn't I said, "Okay." I knew what they'd spoken about. It had taken Maddy less than seventy-two hours to spill the beans.

"This is some kind of prank isn't it? You're playing a joke on your sister and it just got out of hand."

"Um, okay, sure. It's a prank. Nothing to worry about." Hey, she'd thrown me a life preserver; I grabbed it.

"Good. Call your sister and explain that to her."

That wasn't going to work. Maddy knew I was gay and there wasn't a way she could un-know that. If I called her and said, "Hey it was all a joke, gotcha!" she wouldn't believe it.

"You know Maddy, Mom, she's going to believe what she wants to believe."

"It doesn't matter what she believes. Call her and tell her the truth. Tell her you're not gay."

And then it didn't feel much like a life preserver, at all. Now it felt like an anchor, pulling me down again. "You know Mom, I can call Maddy and tell her it was prank. I can tell her I'm not gay if you want. But...let's not call it the truth, okay? Because it's not the truth."

"You're *not* gay."

"We can pretend I'm not. That's okay."

"Dougie, I'm your mother. I would know something like this. You were always such a boy."

"I'm still a boy, Mom."

"But..." She went silent. I knew she was struggling to understand. "There are a lot of gay guys in nursing. I'm not unsophisticated. You're not like them, Dougie. I mean, they're all such girls."

"The ones you know about."

"Well...I don't go around asking about people's sex lives."

"Yes, you do. All the time. You ask people if they're married. Or dating. Or trying to have babies."

"That's different."

"Is it? You know how babies are made. You know what married people do."

"Married couples do a lot more than just have sex."

"So do gay guys."

"Wait...there is this one guy at work. He talks about his partner, Terry. They're trying to have a child with a surrogate. I thought he meant Terry with an 'i', but...

"Mom...'partner.'"

"I thought it meant they weren't married. You know, this explains some of the confused looks he's given me." She got quiet for a moment. "So, you're really gay?"

"Yes, Mom, I'm really gay."

"This is going to take some getting used to. Why didn't you tell me before now?"

"Because of Dad."

"What about your Dad?"

"His heart."

Where had she been? I wondered.

"Honestly, you and your sister have blown this all out of proportion. It was a minor heart attack and your father's health is excellent now."

"Please, Mom, don't tell him."

"Fine, you can tell him yourself. How about Saturday night? I'll make dinner. You're not a secret vegetarian, too, are you?"

"Um, I'm not ready to tell Dad." I really didn't buy the 'it was just a small heart attack' line. I wondered if his doctor would answer questions if I called.

"You can't wait, Dougie. You know I'm bad at secrets."

She was terrible at secrets. She'd announced to the entire world that Maddy was five months pregnant when she got married—even after helping her choose a dress that would disguise that fact. She also let the cat out of the bag when Maddy got pregnant with Leland, claiming that she didn't really understand email distribution lists and hadn't even known she'd made one. Luckily, I'd shared very few secrets with her. Except, of course, my prom. She'd asked who I wanted to take, so I picked out the prettiest girl in the class expecting she'd turn me down. Unfortunately, my mother knew her mother, so I spent my senior prom dancing with a very pretty girl I didn't want to be dancing with while half the boys in my class hated my guts and the other half egged me on.

Crap. I was going to have to come out to my dad on Saturday.

CHAPTER NINE

I wanted to kill Dog. It was one thing to abandon me in the middle of a restaurant and not come back, but then to send an email to my boss getting me fired—I mean, what did I ever do to him? Why would he treat me like that? Okay, so right before I killed him, I would ask some questions.

All day Friday I suffered through a bad hangover. I'd stayed at The Bird until closing, which meant I'd gotten really, really sloshy. Larry Lamour sat with me until eleven. He said a lot of things that I didn't quite get or didn't exactly care about, but before he left he said this one thing that just got to me. He said, "One of the hardest things in life is truly being yourself. Most of us are the person we think we should be, the person who pleases our parents, the person who pleases our friends. So few of us are truly who we are."

I was completely drunk when he said it, so I had a little trouble working it out. But it stuck with me. I was thinking about it when I crawled into bed. I was thinking about it when I woke two hours later and puked my guts out. And I was thinking about it while I stumbled over to the coffee shop to get a latte.

Was I who I was because that's who I was? Or was I who I was because that's who I thought I should be? Did I act like a big old queen because that's what I thought gay guys were like or was I just naturally queeny?

Oh my Gawd, I have to stop, I thought. I had to focus on finding a job. I had to have money coming in. This was exactly the wrong time to be questioning my very identity; self-examination would be pointless if I was living on the street.

Finally, in the late afternoon, I showered. I shaved. I dressed as conservatively as possible: pressed baby blue shirt, khakis. Gawd, I hated khakis—it had taken nearly an hour for me to find them, crammed in the back of a drawer behind a half dozen Jägermeister T-shirts—but they were perfect for job interviews. Not that I had any set up. My plan was to walk around the neighborhood looking for "help wanted" signs and put in applications at places I'd like to work even if there weren't any openings just then.

There were actually a ton of restaurants and bars within a half-mile of my apartment. I assumed Bob would give me a good reference, though I wondered what he'd say about why I didn't work there anymore. It might be a good idea to avoid Bob all together. I found my phone and called Carlos.

"Carlotta, I need a favor."

"Anything Lynette."

"I'm going out to look for a job."

"Oh, you are ambitious. If I were you, I'd be laying in bed hoping for the world to end." I'd actually done that for three hours. It was tragic and boring.

"I'm going to give people your number as a reference."

"All right. I can say nice things about you. Let me practice. He's so, so nice. He's attentive. He's such a hard worker."

"I need you to say you're Bob."

"Oh, really?"

"Yes. Say you're Bob and that I still work at The Bird. Say you're upset that I might leave."

"Sure, I can do that. 'This is Bob Grotolli and Lionel still works at The Bird.'" If you knew Bob, you'd know his impersonation was horrible; if you knew Carmen Miranda, you'd think you were talking to her. Fortunately, Bob was kind of reclusive and no one knew who Carmen Miranda was anymore.

"Thanks, Carlotta. You're a peach."

For the next two hours, I walked the length of Broadway from Alamitos to Redondo, about thirty blocks, twice. I filled out applications at three restaurants and four bars. I didn't find any openings. That meant, I had to widen the search. The sun was going down when I started down Fourth Street.

A place called the V-Bar, which was a small, boxy gray building, had a sign in the front window that said: Bartender wanted. All the other places I'd left applications were places I'd feel pretty comfortable working at, but they had no jobs. This place had a job, but I was pretty certain I was not going to feel comfortable.

I walked by it, deciding not to go in. There was no way a girl like me was going to get hired in a place like that. I might as well not even try. Then I kicked myself—in the shins until I squealed—metaphorically. If I didn't go places I might not be welcome, I'd never go anywhere. And, unfortunately, going home and pulling the blankets over my head was not going to pay the rent.

Turning around, I walked back to V-Bar and went inside.

The bar was dark as night, the only real light coming from a digital jukebox stuck on the wall. There were peanut shells on the floor. I think they were mainly there so no one ever had to mop it. The place smelled of beer and piss. I squinted and saw a woman behind the bar in a leather vest, jeans and not much else. She looked sexy, but it was the kind of sexy that could knock you on your ass if you said the wrong thing.

I made a snap decision, one that I hoped would have positive results.

Taking a deep breath, I widened my stance and stomped up to the bar. "Hey," I said. "Saw your sign." I kept my voice low and tried to sound dumb. I glanced around the bar, it was filling up with the after work crowd; almost twenty men, all burly and rough around the edges, and two women both trussed up in skimpy dresses and push-up bras. Okay, so maybe applying for a job at V-Bar wasn't a good idea, but it was an idea, and I desperately needed one of those.

The barmaid looked me up and down, walked over to the register, slipped out a piece of paper from a folder and brought it over and laid it on the bar in front of me. An application. I started to say, "Could I have a pen, please?" but checked myself. In my lowered voice, I asked, "Gotta pen?"

She pulled a pen out of a glass and slid it over to me. "I'm Pepper Dees."

It took every ounce of restraint not to scream, *Pepper! You mean like Angie Dickinson in Police Woman. Oh my Gawd!* Instead, I just nodded and said, "Leo."

Leo? Was that even short for Lionel? Lee, definitely. Nell, if you were tormenting me in high school. But Leo?

I couldn't remember. Anyway, it was too late. My name was now Leo.

"I'll give you a minute with that, Leo," Pepper said then walked away.

Quickly, I filled out the information at the top of the application. Name. Social. Phone. Address. That stuff was easy. Then I got to work experience. I couldn't put down The Bird as my most recent job. That wasn't going to work. I was going to have to get creative. In fact, the rest of the application was pure fiction. No working as a hair stylist, no beauty school, no GED. I mean, if I was lying I might as well finish high school. And throw on a year of junior college, what the heck, right?

When I was done I tipped my head at Pepper. She came down the bar and gave my application the once over. Then she stared at me again. She liked staring, I could tell. I tried not to flinch.

"Over-pour or under-pour?"

"Over-pour early so they stay, under-pour late so they go away." Lance had explained that to me once. Though I think he over-poured anyone he wanted to sleep with all night long.

"Harvey Wallbanger?"

"Vodka, Galliano, orange juice." I'd never bartended in my life, but two years as a cocktail waiter at The Bird did teach me what was in what drink.

"Long Island Iced Tea?"

"Tequila, gin, vodka, rum, Triple Sec, bar mix, splash of cola."

"Pink lady?"

Shit. Did she have my number? Was she calling me a name? I kept my cool. "In this place? You fuckin' kidding me? Do you even have a blender back there?"

She burst into a laugh. "Okay. I think I like you. If your references check out, I'll give you a call."

I said, "Cool" and lumbered out of the bar.

As soon as I got outside, my hands flew into the air and I squealed. I'd just applied for a job in a straight bar; and not just any straight bar, a dive, an absolute dive. Not that I expected to get the job. Only one of my references was going to answer, but at least I'd had an adventure.

I got my phone out and found a number. A moment later, I asked, "Carlotta, how's your butch voice?"

"What cha talkin' bout, man. I am fuckin' butch. Twenty-four seven."

It was okay. Not as good as he thought but okay.

"You're probably going to get a phone call. Remember that restaurant, Café Pistachio that used to be on Broadway down by Redondo?"

"The one that had the suspicious fire last month."

"Yeah. You used to manage it."

"I did? I didn't start the fire, did I? I can't go to prison, I'm too pretty."

"When you get the call, tell them I used to work for you and that I'm a great bartender. And act really butch when you do it."

"Oh, you want me to lie."

"Of course I want you to lie. That's what friends are for."

###

My parents still live in the house I grew up in. It's in the Bixby neighborhood, and began as a simple two-bedroom ranch. Now, after three additions it is a four-bedroom house with family room, den and workshop. There are big old trees turning the whole neighborhood shady, and speed bumps every two hundred feet. I hoped my parents hadn't noticed me driving around the block about five times working up the courage to go in.

I'd just cracked a PBR with my dad when he said to me, "Funny. Someone with a truck just liked yours was circling the block a few minutes ago."

I kicked myself. I knew my sixty-year-old, retired Dad didn't have much to do but look out the window every few minutes. In the future, I needed to circle another block if I was afraid to come in.

"Something's going on," he said. We were sitting alone in the family room. The sixty-inch TV was tuned to ESPN but the sound was off. It looked like some kind of show about last year's football season. A recap getting the fans ready for the season about to start.

"Your mom has made herself scarce. That means you've got something to tell me. Something I'm not going to like."

Despite the beer my mouth was incredibly dry. How was I going to say this? Should I try to soften the blow some how? Or should I just say it? Why hadn't I asked my mom how I should do it? Why hadn't I read about coming out on the Internet? There had to be a right way to do it. And I knew that whatever way was the right way, I wasn't going to find it on my own.

"I've been expecting this for a long time," my dad said.

"You have?"

He nodded very solemnly. "What the girl's name?"

"What?"

"The girl you've knocked up. What's her name? She's keeping the baby, isn't she? If she weren't, you'd have just taken care of things and kept your mother and I in the dark. Are you going to marry her? It's the right thing to do, you know. Even Arthur married your sister and he's not half the man you are."

"There's no girl, Dad."

"Oh. Well, you've done something wrong. I recognize the look on your face. I've been seeing it there since you were three years old."

"There's never going to be a girl, Dad."

His face fell and he turned a bit white. He was beginning to understand. He looked sad rather than angry. I had a brief moment of hope that this might actually be—

"Is it cancer?"

"Is what cancer?"

"Whatever's wrong with your...man bits."

"My bits are fine, Dad."

"Well then, what on earth is this conversation about? I don't think I've ever had a conversation like this with you. Ever. Just come out with it, for God's sake. Tell me what's wrong with you."

"I'm gay."

He squinted his eyes at me. Something he did a lot at the TV, particularly when he watched the news. His face twitched. Softly, under his breath and with some regret, he said, "You're not a man."

"No, Dad, I—"

"Get out." This in his angry-calm voice. A voice that had terrified me all my life.

"I, uh, we should talk."

"No. I said get out."

I got up and without stopping in the kitchen to say good-bye to my mom I walked out of the house. Sitting in my truck, I tried to think what I should do. I should call someone. I shouldn't be alone. Couldn't be alone. I took my phone and thought about who I wanted to call. I wanted to call Lionel. But that was stupid. Incredibly stupid. I didn't have his number and he wouldn't want to hear from me if I did. Shit, it had been a crappy week. I couldn't remember when I'd had such a crappy week.

I called Fetch. "Hey, what's going on tonight?"

"Tim and a bunch of us are going to The Pub."

"What time?"

"Ten, ten-thirty."

"Okay. See you there."

I clicked off. I had about three hours. Well, I hadn't gotten the dinner I was expecting so I should probably get something to eat. As I started the truck I had to laugh a little. It was the second time that week I'd gone to dinner and not eaten.

I was deciding between In-N-Out or Chronic Taco when my phone rang. My dashboard told me it was my mom. I clicked the call on.

"Hey."

Her voice was kinda low. "I'm in the garage. I'm letting your father stew for a few minutes. Now don't worry, everything will be fine. Just give me a little time to work on him."

A ball of emotion inflated in my chest. I pulled over to the curb just to be safe. I don't think I'd cried since I was eight. So if was going to do that, I didn't want to be driving. Crying while driving was a skill I'd never picked up.

"Dad was pretty upset."

"That's the way your father is with everything. He starts with anger and then works his way through his emotions until he gets to good guy."

"I don't know if this is going to work that way."

"I said I'll work on him, and I will."

"Mom, you're not exactly thrilled about this yourself."

"I've had a very busy twenty-four hours. And I've come a long way. Last night I was on the same shift with Juan Hernandez. He's a gay, and he explained a lot of things to me. He told me all about bears and otters and wolves and cubs and polar bears, and—oh my God you boys like your wild animals, don't you?"

"Oh Jesus... Do we have to have this conversation?"

"And then this morning I went onto the Internet to do some research. You boys also really like your porn, don't you? Every single Google search—"

"Mom!"

"Oh please. I've been a nurse for thirty years. I know people have sex and I know they have it in unusual ways. Now there is one thing I really have to say to you. Household items are *not* sex toys. If you need to use something like that, buy it at sex shop. It's much safer. I'm sure you've heard the horror stories of young men coming into the ED with, well, various items—"

"Mom!"

"What? Those stories are true. So I want you to be careful. I want you to be safe. You are safe, aren't you? And what about Truvada? Have you considered that?"

"Mom! Go back inside and make sure Dad's okay."

"Oh your father's fine. I just fixed him a scotch on the rocks and laced it with a half milligram of lorazepam. He'll be asleep in about an hour."

"Um, isn't that dangerous?"

"You don't think it's the first time I've done it, do you? Look, let's get back to what's important. Are you a relationship-oriented gay? Or are you more into hook-ups?"

CHAPTER TEN

On Sunday morning, Pepper called to tell me I had the job at V-Bar and that I started on Tuesday. I'd be working days, five days a week, Tuesday through Saturday. She assured me it was easy enough. Mostly draft beers, shots and the occasional mixed drink. I might get on nights eventually, that's where the money was, but for now she'd start me out on days.

It was such an amazing relief to have a new job, and so quickly. I was proud of myself for not screaming with delight when she gave me the job. I mean, while I was still on the phone. Of course, the minute I hung up I screamed with delight and jumped about. As soon as I caught my breath, I started to feel a tad freaked out that I was going to have to pretend to be straight eight hours a day, five days a week. Maybe I'd just keep the job until I got something better. I was also worried about how long I could actually pass. I mean, basically I had to speak in monosyllables and keep my hands in my pockets so they didn't flutter about.

After a quick shower, I called Carlos and begged him to take me shopping for an hour or two before he had to go into The Bird for his Sunday shift. Since I had a job, my severance pay was now extra cash. I decided to be good, and put half of it into my car fund and splurge with the other half.

When Carlos pulled up in front of my apartment building, I climbed in. "How is Frida feeling today?"

"She's a little under the weather."

I offered him a twenty, saying, "Will this make her feel better?"

"Oh you shouldn't give me money. You need every penny you have."

"No, I got that job. Thank you, by the way. Obviously, she bought whatever you said."

"Lynette, no one called me."

"Are you serious?"

"Of course, I'm serious. You know I only lie about sex."

It was a little odd. She'd said she was going to check my references, but she hadn't and she'd hired me anyway. I decided to put it out of my mind and focus on one of the most important things in life: shopping.

"I want to go to a mall," I told Carlos.

"I'm not sure Frida will make it all the way to Fascist Island."

Fashion Island in Newport Beach was a good forty-five minutes away, so I had to agree with him. There was a closer mall in Costa Mesa and an even closer mall in Westminster. The Westminster mall was low end, but about as far as we dared take Frida. In fact, we didn't even have to get on the freeway to get there.

Twenty-five minutes later, we were in the men's department at Macy's. V-Bar wasn't the kind of bar where I'd need nice clothes. Jeans were fine. I picked out a very simple, boring pair of 501s. I made sure they were a tiny bit too big, even though it nearly killed me. Tight jeans were so much more flattering to my ass. And so much a part of who I was. I felt like a fraud in baggy jeans.

The thing Larry Lamour had said about being yourself popped into my head, but I immediately rejected it. This was different. Not being me was a financial necessity.

Carlos and I went to the sale rack and started picking out T-shirts with funky things written on them. Even though I hated T-shirts with logos, I picked out several Nike T-shirts, some superhero shirts—Batman, Superman, Captain America—and a plain black shirt with little pink flamingos all over it.

"You cannot wear pink flamingos to a straight bar," Carlos said.

"Oh, I know. That one's for me. I have a pair of pink shorts that it would work with and it's only ten dollars. And if I'm buying clothes, I have to buy at least one thing I actually like."

"You know, Lynette, if you're going to wear all those Nike shirts, you should maybe own a pair of Nikes."

"Really? Do I have to?"

"I think so."

We went over to the shoe department, piled the things I'd already picked onto a chair and went over to the wall of sneakers. "Oh, Carlotta, look they have red Nikes."

"Step away from the red shoes. You need black Nikes. Nothing else will do."

He picked out a pair that was forty percent off and completely uninteresting. *Well*, I thought, *at least they're cheap*. The clerk got us a pair in my size and I tried them on. They fit. My feet looked like they belonged to a stranger, but the sneakers fit. The clerk rang me up. All together I'd spent almost two hundred dollars on clothes

I mostly didn't care for. That was depressing. That was almost my entire clothing budget for a year.

As Carlos and I began to make our way out of the store, we walked by women's shoes. I stopped dead in my tracks. On the front display was the most amazing pair of red pumps. They had a tiny bit of platform on the sole, five-inch heels and an open toe. They were also on sale, fifty percent off, making them a scandalously cheap fifty dollars. I shoved my bags at Carlos. I had to try them on. They were practically calling my name. Picking up the shoe I went looking for the clerk. When I found her, hovering near the register, I said, "I'd like to try these in a twelve."

She didn't bat an eye. I suspected it wasn't her first time at this particular rodeo. The South Bay area was crawling with drag queens. They performed at Hamburger Mary's, the Executive Suite, Waves, and a half dozen other bars, not to mention what was going on in L.A. Somewhere in the county there was a drag show every night of the week. Those girls had to buy shoes somewhere.

"Lynette, what are you doing?"

"I'm trying on a pair of shoes."

"You can't wear those to your new job."

"I'm not working at a straight bar twenty-four seven."

"So, where are you planning to wear them?"

"I have a few ideas."

"Are we going to look at ladies dresses next?"

"Carlotta, you know I don't do drag. I do gender-fuck."

###

On Sunday morning I was hungover. Part of me

didn't want to play softball. I didn't want to see Chuckie; he was an asshole. I'd known that before he tried to get Lionel fired. The only real difference was now I knew he was a *major* asshole. Of course, I also didn't want to see Lionel at The Bird when the game was over. After I dumped him at Massie's, I was pretty sure I was as big an asshole as Chuckie and I didn't need to be reminded of that.

My phone had been ringing all morning and I'd been ignoring it. Finally, I checked my messages. There were three calls from Maddy. Obviously, she wanted to know how things went with Dad. I was pretty sure she already knew. She'd probably talked to my mom at least six times before she'd even tried me once. I decided she had enough information about my life for now. And, if my mother was sharing everything she'd found out, a lot more than she needed.

There was also a message from my dad. That one I listened to. He was ordering me, in no uncertain terms, to join them at church. That was not going to happen; partly because church was already over. My mother was probably going to try to call that progress. His insisting I go to church with them. He'd moved from "you're not a man" to "hate the sin, not the sinner." I wouldn't call it progress, though. It seemed more like a lateral move.

Of course, when it was time for the game I completely sucked. I might have been able to play through my hangover. I might have been able to play through the distraction of the mess with my family. But what I couldn't play through was Chuckie Cooper.

The field we used was in Tustin, where things are a bit more spread out. The city supported a large green park that somehow stayed green no matter how severe the drought got. The field was basic: tall fence behind the batter, benches beyond that, a small set of bleachers for anyone who showed up to watch. We did have a few regular spectators. Boyfriends and husbands. Occasionally parents, but not often. While we were still getting organized, unpacking our equipment from Tim's SUV and putting together a lineup, and generally catching up after the week, Chuckie called everyone together to make an announcement.

"Finally, he's going to tell us how we get out of this slump," Simon said.

But that wasn't what he had planned. "On Monday I sent you all an email asking that you contact Bob Grottoli at The Bird and complain about the way I was disrespected by one of his employees last week. I'm so moved that each and every one of you did just that. It means a lot to me that you guys have my back."

What was he talking about? I wondered. I didn't send an email. Why did he think I sent an email?

"And you'll be happy to know that when we go to The Bird after the game, that particular employee will not be there."

Crap. He did it. He got Lionel fired. And if someone told Lionel that everyone on the team— Lionel must hate me. He thinks I deliberately abandoned him in a restaurant and then got him fired. Okay, I did sort of abandon him on purpose. But I didn't get him fired. Crap.

When Chuckie was done with his speech everyone went back to doing ineffective warm-ups. I walked over to him.

"Hey man, you know I didn't send an email."

"Yeah, I figured mine got stuck in your spam folder or something, so I went ahead and let Bob know how you felt."

"But you don't know how I feel."

"I figured you felt...you know, the right way about it."

"I don't. I mean... You called Lionel names. You didn't tip him. And then you got him fired. The right way to feel about it is that you're an asshole."

"So you're saying you don't have my back."

"I'm saying I don't think you're a good person."

"Well, that's not having my back."

The game was a disaster. As team captain, Chuckie always put himself on the lineup as starting pitcher. Tim was a better pitcher, but that didn't matter to Chuckie. He always started. I was on second base like usual. Every time a hit came toward Chuckie he'd grab the ball, then turn around and throw it my way whether there was a runner coming or not. And not just throw it my way. Throw it at me. Aiming right at my head. The whole thing was kinda ironic, because in general he was throwing a crap game. He walked two or three guys each inning and we went down 10 to 2.

After the game, Fetch and Tim rode with me back to The Bird.

"We have to find a way to start winning," Tim said.

"Definitely, we have to do something," Fetch agreed.

"It's too bad Chuckie is so against Linda Sue playing with us," I said.

"Oh man, that would be amazing," Fetch said.

"It would be."

"What's going on with you and Chuckie?" Fetch asked from the backseat.

"It looked like he was trying to kill you," Tim said from the front.

"He was. I didn't send an email to Bob Grottoli, so he put my name in for me. I told him that wasn't okay with me. I told him he was in the wrong."

"You told Chuckie he was wrong about something?"

"That's not a great idea."

"But he *was* wrong," I pointed out.

"Doesn't matter."

"He's gunning for you now."

"And everyone's gonna let him?"

"You bet your ass. It was nice playing with you, though."

"Maybe you can find a different team next year."

"You guys are just going to let him run me off the team?"

"Anyone who crosses him has to pay. I don't want to cross him."

"You know, maybe it would be a good idea if you didn't come to The Bird today."

The last thing in the world I wanted to do was drink, but there was no way I was going to let Chuckie run me off. And if I didn't show up at The Bird, he'd think that's exactly what he'd done. That's what everyone would think. They'd all think he'd run me off and none of them would ever dare stand up to him.

For the good of the team, I was going to have to get drunk.

CHAPTER ELEVEN

I decided to wait until six-thirty before making my grand entrance. I'd spent the entire afternoon primping and polishing and plotting. When I got them home, the red heels were still fabulous. They looked great on (I'd taken a mirror off the wall and set it on the floor to be sure) and, for five-inch heals, were almost comfortable. I picked out a skin-tight pair of jeans to wear with them and then rolled the hem turning them into impromptu capris. I wore a nice, crisp, tailored black shirt that I accented with a rhinestone spray that had been my grandmother's, then my mother's, then mine. I couldn't help thinking even my family heirlooms were fake, but you know what? As the great Doris Day once said, "Que sera, sera." Life is too short to wait around for real diamonds. Deciding against full makeup—it really was very uncomfortable—I brushed on a tiny bit of mascara, moussed my hair into a drama swoop, and I was ready to go.

My plan was to show up and find a way to humiliate the bejesus out of Dog. I was pretty sure he hadn't told any of his softball buddies that he'd hooked up with me. So, all I really had to do was saunter into the bar, shimmy over to Dog and plant one big, motherfucking French kiss on him. And if I had enough time, maybe I'd stick a fork into the back of Chuckie Cooper's hand. All right, stabbing people is illegal and can get a person sent to prison. I knew I had to skip that. But it was so, so very tempting.

It was still light when I walked the two and a half blocks from my apartment to The Bird. It was a bummer that my new job was fourteen blocks away. That was a long way to walk but too close to justify a cab. And, of course, I hated taking the bus since I was convinced everyone on it wanted to kill me.

In the restaurant section, there were only a smattering of customers, the bar however, was almost full. I saw Carlos scampering about trying to fill as many drink orders as he could. I scanned the room and found Andrew lurking next to a table by the piano. A pretty girl of twenty-something was sitting there. Andrew was pouting extra hard, which I think was his version of flirting.

The Birdmen surrounded the bar. I looked for Dog, planning to walk right over and make a spectacle, but I saw Chuckie first. And without thinking it through changed my plan. I walked up to Chuckie and tapped him on the shoulder. He turned around and looked me up and down, from my red heels to my mascara-ed eyes.

"Care to buy a girl a drink?"

"Fuck you."

"I hear you got me fired. You see the problem with that, Chuckie, is that now I'm just another customer and you can't do anything about it."

"Get away from me."

"I'm two feet away from you. It's a crowded bar. This is where I'm going to stand."

"I said get the fuck away from me."

"Make me."

Chuckie gave me a hard shove. I was kind of expecting it, but I hadn't thought through what it was like to be shoved while wearing five-inch heels. I teetered backward, my right ankle bent and probably sprained, then I began to fall like a tree in the forest. I was actually surprised no one yelled timber.

And then, surprisingly, I did not land on the floor. Someone caught me. Thank Gawd. I looked up to see whose arms I'd just fallen into—it was Dog. Not thank Gawd. In fact, no thank you very much Gawd. I struggled to my feet, struggled to stay standing on my now excruciatingly sore right ankle. I pushed away from Dog, looking from him to Chuckie and back again.

"Great. Caught between two assholes."

And because I didn't think it likely I'd be able to come up with a better exit line. I hobbled out of the bar. When I got to the corner of Broadway and Gaviota, I stopped. Even though I only lived a few blocks away, there was no way I was going to be able to walk home. I took off my heels and tried walking a few feet barefoot. No, not going to happen.

Fuck. Fuck. Fuck. There wasn't anyone I could call to come and give me a ride for two blocks. Carlos was working, so he couldn't do it. When it came right down to it, most of the other people I knew were little more than acquaintances and weren't at all likely to come rescue me on a Sunday evening.

"Do you need help?"

I turned to see Dog standing there. *Fuck*, I thought. The only way I could think to get home was to accept his help. Or call Uber and have the driver bitch because I only wanted to go a couple of blocks.

"Sure. I could use a hand. It's two and a half blocks. Can you manage that? Or will you disappear after the first block?"

"I want to explain about that."

"Oh please, go right ahead."

I gave him my best Joan Crawford stare—which he totally ignored. He grabbed my arm and put it around his shoulder. Slowly, we started to walk/hop back to my apartment.

"Just as our entrées arrived my parents were seated across the restaurant."

"Oh. And you're not out to them."

"I am now."

"They saw you?"

"No, it was sort of a coincidence. I called my sister to find out why they were there, they never go out, and she roped me into dinner with my ex-fiancée. Jennifer, Jen had had lunch with my ex-boyfriend, so the cat was out of the bag. My sister told my mother and then my mother made me tell my dad."

"Chatty family. And they all hate you now?"

"My dad said I wasn't a man."

I wanted to go on hating Dog, but I felt bad; I knew what it was like to disappoint a father. "That's a hard thing to hear."

"My mom thinks he'll get over it. But I don't know."

"It doesn't matter if he gets over it. What matters is that you do. You need to forgive yourself."

"For what? For being gay?"

"For not being who your dad wants you to be."

###

When we got to Lionel's place I tried to walk inside with him, but he stopped me. "I can take it from here. Thanks."

"Oh, um, I thought we could talk some more."

"Yeah, I know exactly what you thought."

"No, I, well not really." My cold was gone and I had thought, if things went well, we might...

"Look, you had a reasonably good excuse for dumping me at a restaurant and you do get points for paying the bill. Sorry about the extra seventy bucks I spent on desert. But you also sent an email to my boss asking that I be fired, so I really don't feel like—"

"I didn't do that. Chuckie said I did, but I didn't. I think it's terrible that he got you fired."

He shrugged. "Oh, well...no, biggie. I've already got another job."

"If it's not a big deal, then why are you mad at me?"

"Principle."

Then he took out his keys and between the screen door, putting the key into the lock, holding a pair of red heels in one hand and standing on his good foot, Lionel ended up on the floor in a heap just inside his apartment. He looked up at me. "All right, fine. You can come in."

I helped him off the floor and onto his sofa. Grabbing one of the star-shaped throw pillows off the white velvet couch, I put it under his foot on the coffee table. Then I put my hands on his ankle.

"What are you doing?"

"I'm going to check to make sure it isn't broken."

"No. Don't do that."

"Relax. I'm a health professional."

"You run a treadmill."

"And I'm trained in first aid and advanced cardio-vascular life support."

"My heart's fine."

"Plus my mother's a nurse."

"Oh, well, in that case. Go right ahead."

I knew he was being sarcastic, but I took the opening and gently felt around his ankle, carefully turning it in each direction. "Yeah, that feels like it's just a sprain."

"Just a sprain? It hurts like hell."

"We need to wrap it. Do you have an ace bandage?"

"Why would I have an ace bandage?"

"I've got one in my truck." I handed him the remote to his TV. "Stay right here. Don't move."

My truck was on the other side of The Bird, so I had to walk about four blocks. As I did, I checked my phone. I'd had the ringer off since noon. There were three more calls from my sister and none from my dad. That was good—or not good. I didn't know which. There was also a call from Fetch. He left a message asking where I'd gone. Since I'd given him and Tim a ride, I had to call him back.

"Dude, where'd you go? Chuckie is talking shit about you to everyone." I could hear Larry Lamour playing in the background.

"I had to help Lionel home. He twisted his ankle."

"Lionel? Why would you help him?"

"He couldn't walk."

"But, Chuckie hates him. You're just making things worse." I could hear him lean away from the phone and talk to someone. "Tim says maybe you'd better not come back here."

"I'm *not* coming back there."

"And you can tell your friend Lionel they've banned him from the bar."

"They've what?"

"Yeah, Bob came in right afterward and Chuckie threw a hissy fit."

"Wait, Chuckie shoves Lionel and Lionel is the one who gets banned?"

"Well, he was kind of asking for it."

"Whatever. I mainly just wanted to let you guys know I'm not giving you a ride home. You can find someone else to give you a ride, right?"

"Yeah, sure." He said something to Tim again. Then, "Yeah, we'll be fine."

I almost hung up, but then I stopped. "So Fetch, what kind of person are you?"

"What? What do you mean by that?"

"I mean, Chuckie is bullying the whole team while you and everyone else let him."

There was a long pause. I could hear some applause in the background for Larry Lamour. I imagined for a moment it was for me, since I'd finally said what was on my mind. Then Fetch said, "I gotta go, man."

He clicked off and I put my phone into my back pocket. I figured that was the end of me and gay softball. That sucked. I'd really enjoyed being on the team. I felt like I fit. I was going to miss that feeling. Then I had a really sad thought. Maybe that's why the guys were all willing to put up with Chuckie. Because they wanted to fit in.

I got to my truck and pulled out the first aid kit from behind the seat. One of the reasons I carried it was because of the team. Lionel's was not the first sprained ankle I'd dealt with. I grabbed the Ace bandage and instant ice pack. No reason to bring the whole kit.

Then I realized something else. I'd chosen Lionel over the team. That's kinda what Fetch was saying to me. If he knew I'd had sex with Lionel, he'd have come right out and said it. And it was kinda true. I *was* choosing Lionel over the team. And it wasn't just because Chuckie was an asshole. It was because I liked Lionel. I didn't always understand what he was talking about or why he liked the things he liked, but I liked to listen to the things he said.

And I wanted to keep listening.

CHAPTER TWELVE

While Dog was gone, I decided to have sex with him. I mean, he wasn't the son of a bitch I thought he was and I couldn't walk so there wasn't much else to do. It was, in my humble opinion, a very practical decision. Not that sex is a default position with me, though it was close. Plus, Dog was fucking sexy. And good in bed. I couldn't think of a reason not to have sex with him. And I did try.

When he got back, he got busy. He wrapped my ankle and then smashed up a chemical ice pack so it would work.

"You're going to need to stay off it for a few days."

"Really? Shit, I start my new job on Tuesday."

"Okay, well, stay off it until then. Keep it wrapped. Ice it every few hours. Take lots of analgesics."

"Anal whats?" I resisted batting my eyes. Well, I tried to resist.

"Hah-hah. I've heard that one before. Aspirin. Ibuprofen. Acetaminophen."

"Oh. That's not as much fun as what I was imagining."

"They're going to be a lot of fun once the pain sets in."

"Are you implying that the pain hasn't set in?"

"No. It hasn't. It will be bad tomorrow, then it will get better each day. I mean, if you go to work on Tuesday, you're going to need to come right home and elevate it again. Ice it, too." He stood there awkwardly. "Well, I should get going."

"You don't have to."

"But you didn't want to let me in."

"I changed my mind. Stick around. We'll get a pizza. Watch a movie or something." It was the 'or something' I was most interested in. "Sit down, okay?"

He looked at my yellow chair and decided to sit on the couch. But not too close. "So, what's the deal with those?" he asked, pointing at my beautiful red heels which were now sitting on the coffee table next to my wounded ankle. "Are you like a drag queen?"

"Oh Gawd, no. Drag queens are performers. I don't want to perform. I don't want to walk a runway, or lip sync, or tell jokes. I just like to wear pretty shoes."

"Why?"

"I like the way they make my ankles look. And I like to fuck with people."

"Yeah, I noticed...the part where you mess with people, I mean. That's not always a good idea."

I shrugged.

"Bad things can happen."

And they had, but I wasn't in the mood to think much about that. "Bad things happen anyway. I might as well have the satisfaction of knowing why."

He looked worried for a moment, then asked, "Have you always been...this way?"

"You don't have to be careful with me. I know what the world is like. No one ever writes 'please be femme' on their Grindr profile, now do they?"

"That wasn't what I was going to ask. I was going to

ask if you've always been, you know, trouble."

I laughed. "Yes. I guess. When I was a kid, I had to make a decision. I could be the kind of wallflower who always got bullied or I could fight back."

"So you fought back and people stopped bullying you?"

"No, I fought back and they kept bullying me. But I felt better about myself."

"You've had a lot of experience with people like Chuckie?"

"Oh yeah. Lots. You'd think things would have gotten better since, you know, I was working in a gay bar. But things just changed from, 'Oh my Gawd, you're a fag,' to, 'Oh my Gawd, you're the wrong kind of fag.'"

"You could...be different."

"You mean butch it up?"

"I guess."

"Why don't you femme it up?"

"It's not really who I am—oh..."

I didn't know why I was being so hard on him. I had just butched it up to get a job at V-Bar, so it wasn't like I couldn't butch it up—although the fact that I managed it had been a tad surprising. So obviously I had no right to be offended that he'd suggested I do what I'd just done. I mean, I didn't want to butch it up all of the time. That sounded exhausting. Truth be told, I had serious doubts as to how long I'd be able to keep it up working at V-Bar. A swish of the hip, a fluttering hand and a few sprinkles of fabulousness, and I'd be looking for a new job.

"They remind me of my mom," I said.

"Who does?"

"The shoes. High heels remind me of my mom. That's part of why I like to wear them."

"Your mom wore heels that high?"

"Well, no, hers were lower. But, you know, I've got to wear what works for me."

I reached over and grabbed him by the collar of his grungy T-shirt, pulling him to me. His lips were warm, dry and incredibly comfortable, like a mattress that wrapped around you. I slipped my arms around his shoulders and pulled him closer. He hugged me close and we lay pressed together on my velvet sofa. I moaned a little, then so did he. Slipping my hands up under his T-shirt, I found his nipples and began to pinch them. I remembered he'd liked that when I did it the night we met. This time though, he pulled away. "Maybe we should take this slow."

"Slow?"

"Yeah. I think you might be worth waiting for."

I pulled him back to me and whispered into his ear. "We've already had sex. It's too late to wait."

"Slow down, then. Whatever. I think you're worth slowing down for."

I stared at him for a long moment. I was tempted to throw him out. He wanted more than just sex. I had serious doubts. If he wasn't going to put out, I should kick him to the curb—but I didn't.

Instead, we ordered pizza.

###

The next morning, I quit the team.

I have a laptop but I don't use it much. I'm not big on games or apps or posting pictures of my dinner. Most of what I do is email and I read that on my phone anyway. Plus, most emails I get are about straight porn and meds for erectile dysfunction. Neither of which I want or have. So, usually there's nothing in my inbox that can't wait. I'd only use my laptop if I was getting serious about something.

Grabbing it off a shelf, I left my apartment to go to Hot Times, a coffee shop around the corner from my place. It's a cute place with sofas, tables, chairs and even some stools to sit on. I got a latte, found a little table, sat down and dug through my email to find the one Chuckie had sent to everyone asking that they get Lionel fired. I decided I'd resign from the team in a reply-all email. That way every one of the guys who signed the petition would get exactly why I was resigning.

Well, I was going to write something, too. I just didn't know what. Whenever I have something important to write or say or even think about, the first thing I do is avoid it completely.

I called my sister.

"Finally," she said, when she picked up. "I've left you a million messages." Seven, she'd left seven messages. In phone calls, seven equals a million.

"Sorry, I had some stuff to do."

"I'll bet. How did it go with Dad?"

"Didn't Mom tell you?"

"Yes, but I want to hear it from you."

"It didn't go so great."

"That's what Mom said. He'll come around."

"That's what Mom said."

"I know. Can you believe her, though? Oh my God, suddenly she's all G-A-Y friendly."

"Kids in the car?"

"I'm dropping them off at preschool. Mom is acting like she never had a bad thing to say about a G-A-Y person in her life. And we know that's not true. She's said some things about the G-A-Ys."

"Maddy, you don't have to spell the word gay. Your children aren't old enough to know what it means."

"But if I wait until they're old enough to know what it means, they'll be old enough to spell."

"Well, there you go."

"Was Dad horrible?"

"He's not pretending he's never said anything bad about gays."

"Oh, I'm sorry."

Then I had an idea. Maybe not a good one, but an idea. "I have to write an email. Do you think—?"

"Seriously? This is like high school when you'd ask me to do your homework." In my defense, she always did it. And I always got B's. "Okay, as long as we can do it at your place. I love my house, but I'm having serious cabin fever."

"Actually I'm at a coffee shop."

"Coffee shop! Oh my God. I haven't been to a coffee shop in, well I don't know how long."

"What are you talking about? You go to Starbucks all the time."

"I go to the drive through window. I don't actually get to go inside. Is it the one by your apartment? The G-A-Y one? Oh my God. You live in the G-A-Y ghetto and go to G-A-Y coffee shops. How did I ever not know you were G-A-Y? I'll be there in twenty minutes."

She clicked off.

While I waited I stared at the screen, rereading the email Chuckie had sent. Well, first I was staring at the replies, having to scroll through the "Okays," the "Will dos" and the "You got it Big Mans." At the bottom was Chuckie's original email.

It read:

Dear Team,

Yesterday, after the game, the flitty little cocktail waiter at The Bird behaved in a rude, disrespectful and thoroughly inappropriate way toward me. As your captain, I hope you'll join me in letting Bob Grottoli, the owner of The Bird, know that sort of behavior cannot be tolerated. We're grateful for his support of the Birdmen, but are also aware that we bring publicity and goodwill to his establishment. Not to mention we spend a good amount of money there each weekend.

Any employee who treats us badly is sabotaging his business and he should not tolerate it. If a team member behaved this badly he would be tossed off the team. We all know that.

Thanks for your support.

Chuckie Cooper

Maddy arrived while I was mulling over how I might say what I wanted to say. She went up to the counter and got herself a soy latte with two caramel pumps. When she got to the table I had her read Chuckie's email.

"Wait, you're on a softball team? Why didn't you say anything?"

"It's a *gay* softball league."

"Does everything come in a gay flavor? Should I have gotten a gay latte?"

I gave her a dirty look. "You're being ridiculous. You can figure out why there are gay sports teams."

"Did you tell Mom you play softball? She needs to tell Dad. You know how he is about team sports. That could solve half your problem right there."

"Could we just write the email?"

She frowned as she read it closely

"So what did the flitty waiter do?" she asked, sipping her coffee drink. "This is good by the way. Gays do everything better."

I closed my eyes and sighed. I knew that someday she'd get bored with the fact that I was gay. I looked forward to that.

"Lionel, that's the waiter's name. He didn't do anything. I mean, he did. He reacted. Chuckie called him nelly and then Lionel said he 'wouldn't mind being called names if Chuckie knew how to tip' and then Chuckie stiffed him."

"Chuckie is a douche."

"Yeah. And then yesterday, even though he'd been fired, Lionel went into the bar and he and Chuckie had words, and Chuckie pushed him, hard. Lionel sprained an ankle. And instead of throwing Chuckie out they banned Lionel."

I was leaving some big things out of that story and the look on my sister's face told me she knew it. I could see her deciding to ignore that.

"Okay, so reply all."

"Done."

"Dear Team." She began. I typed it in. "'An intolerable situation has arisen and I find that I cannot continue with the team.'"

"That doesn't really sound like me."

"If you want to sound like you, why am I here? You can write 'this sucks, I quit' on your own."

I started typing 'An intolerable situation…'

"So do you have a crush on this nelly guy, Lionel?"

"I guess."

"Will I like him?"

"He's, um, interesting."

"That could mean a million things."

"Uh-huh. Let's keep going, I need to send this."

"Okay... 'After an incident that was largely his own fault, Chuckie used his position as captain to coerce the team into requesting that a cocktail waiter at The Bird be fired.' So is that what you like? Effeminate guys?"

"No. I mean, I like him in spite of it."

She thought about it, then said, "Well, at least people won't wonder who's the woman in bed."

"Maddy!"

CHAPTER THIRTEEN

Dog was right. The next day the pain in my ankle was excruciating. When I woke up I hopped to the bathroom and took three aspirin and two Tylenol. Then I hopped back to bed and pulled my comforter over my head. I felt horribly betrayed. Over the years I'd watched dozens of actresses die of terminal film illnesses and barely register pain. Of course, I wasn't terminal, but JESUS FUCK it hurt. Hollywood could have told me there was more to illness than mood lighting and sallow makeup.

I was marginally better by afternoon, so when Dog called me I didn't scream out in pain. He told me not to eat dinner because he was coming over after work to cook for me. I suggested he get takeout instead, but he seemed really interested in cooking. I prayed that meant he could actually cook.

I clicked off before I realized that cooking in my kitchen could be a problem. I'd lavished a lot of attention on my bedroom and the living room, but absolutely none on the kitchen. To me, a kitchen is of limited use. I keep bottled water, beer, wine and leftover takeout containers in the refrigerator. The freezer is filled with goodies from the frozen food section. My microwaving skills are unrivaled. Apart from the microwave, there are only a few other things I can manage in the kitchen. I can make tea, I can do Pop Tarts in the toaster, and I can make Ramen noodles. Basically, I know how to push buttons and boil water. I texted Dog, FYI: NOT A LOT OF KITCHEN GADGETS.

Two hours later, while finishing up an all-day Shirley MacLaine marathon (*The Apartment*, *Terms of Endearment*, *Steel Magnolias* and *The Turning Point*), I realized I should have eaten something the minute Dog called. He wouldn't get off work until seven, which meant he wouldn't get to my place until almost eight, at which point I'd be so hungry I might eat the throw pillow my foot had been resting on all day. But by then it was too late. I was starving and going to stay that way.

I limped to the door when Dog arrived just before eight, as predicted. He had a bag of groceries in each arm. Paper, not plastic. Plastic bags were now illegal, just like cocaine or stabbing your neighbor. Dog didn't think that was a funny joke when I said it, though, so I just hopped after him as he went into my kitchen. I didn't have a kitchen table, so I hoisted myself onto the counter to watch him cook.

He set the groceries on the counter and, with great speed, looked through my refrigerator, opened my drawers and examined the contents of my cabinets. He looked at me and said, "Hmmmm."

"That's a very judgmental sound."

He held up a red pepper and said, "This is a vegetable."

"Darling, I know what vegetables are. They're the things I pick off a pizza before I eat it."

He growled. Joining the pepper on the counter were a zucchini, an onion, garlic, mushrooms, olive oil, a bag of salad greens, some fresh pasta, a package of Italian sausage, a loaf of French bread, a half-pound of butter and a container of parmesan cheese.

"What are you making?"

"It's a sort of pasta primavera with Italian sausage."

I loved sausage and pasta. I hoped that the primavera part wasn't anything too gross.

He'd already found the pot I used to cook Ramen noodles in, now he looked at me and asked, "Do you have a frying pan?"

I shook my head.

"You don't have a frying pan?"

"No, that would imply that I fry things."

"You don't eat fried food?"

"I buy fried food. I don't make it myself."

He looked inside my oven and found the cookie sheet I used when I wanted frozen pizza. If I ever go to college, I plan to do a dissertation on the differences (and similarities) between frozen pizza and delivery pizza. I think it would be fascinating and culturally valuable. And I've certainly done the research.

"I could roast the vegetables. That'll work." Obviously he was talking to himself. To me he said, "Do you have a sharp knife?"

"Yup."

"Where is it?"

"In the bedroom. Between my mattress and box spring. On the right side."

He looked at me curiously for a moment.

"Yes, I'm the sort of girl who is more likely to need a knife in the bedroom than the kitchen."

"Okay, I'll go get the knife."

He walked out of the kitchen. I listened as his footsteps echoed through my apartment. Then imagined him sliding his hand between the mattress and the box spring—

"Be care—"

"Ouch. Frig." I heard him say. Frig, really? Was I having dinner with a boy who didn't use curse words?

When he came back into the kitchen, Dog had his finger in his mouth. That was kind of sexy. The knife in his other hand, not so much.

"Is it bad?" I asked.

"No, it's okay." He rinsed his finger off in the sink and took a good look at it. I didn't ask if he needed a Band-Aid; I didn't have any. Of course, he probably had six different kinds in his truck, if he really needed one. He seemed to decide his finger was okay and set about chopping veggies. Which left it up to me to make small talk.

"So...frig? What's that about? You don't swear?"

"I try not to."

"Good Gawd, why?"

"It's how I was brought up."

Of course, if memory served, the first thing he really said to me was, 'Wanna fuck?' I decided not to bring that up, and instead asked, "Why softball? What is that about?"

"It's not about softball, exactly. I like being on a team. I mean, there's gay basketball and gay flag football and gay hockey. Like I told you, I did football in high school; I figure I've been knocked around enough, though. Even flag football is more than I want to risk. I'm not tall enough for basketball and the hockey team is practically professional, so that kind of leaves softball."

"I hated team sports in high school."

"Yeah, I know."

"What do you mean, you know? You weren't there."

"We had guys who were...like you."

"Femme," I supplied.

"Um, yeah, I guess. Femme. They always got picked last." He chopped and thought. Then, "Maybe that's why I liked it so much. I got picked first or second. That meant I belonged. That I was part of something. That I wasn't alone. I mean, in high school I was pretty afraid people would figure me out. So there was that. Being on a team now, though, well that's kind of amazing. I'm who I am and I'm still part of something. I belong even more than I did in high school. Now I'm really not alone."

He was adorable when he was serious. But I couldn't help teasing him. "And I bet the locker room orgies keep things interesting."

"It's not like that," he blushed, as though he wasn't telling the truth. "I mean, sometimes things happen, but it's not, you know, like a porno."

"Unfortunately, so little of life is..."

I got the vegetables roasted, the pasta made, and tossed a simple salad. We had to eat on Lionel's white sofa since he didn't have any kind of table. That made me glad I hadn't made anything with a red sauce.

Once we were situated, Lionel with his foot up on the coffee table and me perched on the edge of the couch so I didn't spill anything, he said, "It's nice to know you have a feminine side."

"What do you mean?"

"You cook. That's feminine."

Reflexively, I shook my head. "All the great chefs are men."

"Oh, yeah, you're right. Julie Child was kind of butch. And Martha Stewart, well, I wouldn't want to get into a fight with her. She'd cut a bitch."

I could have named at least a half dozen famous male chefs, but decided not to. He'd made his point. Now I wanted to make mine. "My dad taught me to cook. He learned when he was in the Marines. My mom worked when I was a kid, so Dad made most of the meals. My mom was better at the cleaning. That's how they split things up."

"It's not a bad thing to have a feminine side."

"I didn't say it was."

"You're an excellent cook by the way."

"It's a pretty simple dish. I'll make something complicated for you some time." I took a couple bites of my dinner. Even without a frying pan to sauté the veggies in, it had come out pretty decent. "You never told me about your new job?"

"Bartending at the V-Bar on Fourth Street."

"That's a straight bar." As soon as I said it I regretted it, thinking that Lionel might be offended but he wasn't.

"I butched it up to get the job. Of course, I don't know how long I'm going to be able to keep that up."

"Is it that hard to fake it?" I asked.

"Are you faking it?"

"We've already had this conversation."

"Sorry."

We ate silently. Finally, Lionel said, "Maybe you could give me a few pointers on being straight-acting."

"But I don't think about it. I just...do it."

"Stand up."

"I'm eating."

"Please."

I took a quick bite of my dinner and then set the plate on the coffee table. I stood up.

"Further away. Where I can see you."

I walked over near the TV. "What do you want me to do?"

"Just stand."

I stood. He studied me.

"What do you see?" I asked.

"Sit in the yellow chair."

"Do I have to?"

"Okay, that reaction is very straight-acting. And, yes, you have to."

I sat down in the daisy-like chair, leaned forward and put my hands on my knees. "Is this really helping?"

"Sort of. You maintain a really wide stance. Standing, sitting. It's like you think your dick is enormous. I mean, your dick is nice. I like it. I like it a lot. It just doesn't need the kind of clearance you're giving it."

"Should I stop doing that?"

"I don't care. We're worried about me right now."

Lionel struggled up off the sofa, balancing on his good leg. Gingerly, he set his right foot onto the floor. Then he spread his hips.

"I think that's too wide," I said.

"Really?"

"Yeah. You look kinda like a ballet dancer."

He turned his hips back in a bit. Then he walked a few steps and looked back at me.

"You're swinging your hips too much."

"It's my ankle, I'm all off kilter," he said, snappishly.

"It's okay. You can walk however you want."

"No, I'm sorry. I asked for your help." He walked back to the couch, managing to keep his hips stiller this time. Unfortunately his hands were floating at chest height. "Better?"

"Yeah. Watch your hands, though." He put his hands on his hips. "No, don't put them there."

"Okay."

"Say, 'okay man.' And use dude a lot."

"Okay, man. Dude."

"One or the other," I said, softly. I didn't like criticizing him. "Do you really want to do this? There have to be other jobs."

He got back onto the couch and put his foot back onto the coffee table. "I have to be able to get to work without a car. I mean, I'm saving for a car, I just don't have enough for anything that would actually get me from point A to point B." Then he bit his lip and said, "This is going to be a disaster."

I didn't really know what to say to that. It probably *was* going to be a disaster. "I like you. I like you anyway."

I leaned in for a kiss but got pushed away. "You like me *anyway*? You like me despite that I'm a full-on fairy? You like me despite the fact that you don't like who I am? Is that what you're saying?"

"No. I said that I like you."

"*Anyway*. As in even though... You like me, even though you don't."

"That isn't what I meant."

"So, you say things you don't mean?"

"Not on purpose."

It was very uncomfortable. We both just sat there, neither of us eating.

"Should I go?"

"Up to you. But just so you know...we're not going to fuck. *Anyway*."

CHAPTER FOURTEEN

There's a bus that goes down Fourth Street, so I only had to shamble a single block to catch it, then another block from the bus stop to V-Bar. Since I was in my heterosexual disguise (i.e., khakis and a black T-shirt), I only got three or four murderous glares. I arrived just before ten. The bar opened at eleven. When I walked in, all the lights were on and I got to see what the place was like under its normal veneer of casual seediness. And, believe me, it wasn't pretty.

For one thing, the walls were actually army green, except there were places that had been touched up in an army green that didn't quite match the first army green. Through the peanut shells on the floor, I could see there was a scratched and dinged hardwood floor. The bar itself, which was tiled in a forest green tile that, while in the same color family, clashed jarringly with the walls, was surrounded by stools that looked, well, sticky. They weren't. They just looked that way. Like they'd been used for so long it was now impossible to get them truly clean.

"Hey Leo, how's it hanging?" Pepper said when I walked in.

I almost looked over my shoulder to see who she was

talking to. But then I caught myself and said, "Hey, Pepper. It's hanging." I cringed. Is that how straight guys responded to *How's it hanging?* I mean, I wanted to say, *Fine, thank you*, but that seemed weird. And kind of gay.

In the harsh fluorescent light, Pepper looked a good deal older than I'd thought she was. She had to be pushing fifty. Her long hair was dyed black and cut with bangs across her forehead, like a nineteen-sixties Cher. She wore a lot of makeup, never a good look in natural light. That morning she was wearing a flannel shirt over a lacy bustier. She curved in all the places a woman is supposed to, so my bet was she could get any straight guy she wanted from twenty-one to eighty-one.

"What'd you do to your foot?" she asked when I got behind the bar.

"Kicked something I shouldn't have."

"Something or someone?"

I didn't answer. I figured her imagination was a lot tougher than I was. Right away she jumped into training me. Showed me where everything was. Gave me a mini lesson in how to operate the cash register. While doing all that she'd ask the occasional question about my background, to which I gave monosyllabic answers. I wanted to distract her by asking a question, get her to talk about herself and not me. But it was hard to be preverbal and ask questions at the same time. Finally, I went with "Nice place. Yours?" which was straight for *Oh my Gawd, the bar is fabulous, how long have you owned it?*

"There was a real-estate slump in the mid-nineties, right after the Northridge quake. No one wanted to live in Southern California, so everything got very cheap, very fast. I was working as a paralegal then, so I bought a couple of properties, condos that were practically free and this place. At first there was a bar in here called O'Malley's. Irish pub kind of joint."

That explained the myriad greens, I thought. Though it didn't explain why she hadn't redecorated.

"O'Malley retired around Y2K. I tried to find a tenant for a while, then I realized I was tired of lawyers—for some reason they think they're immune to sexual harassment laws—and so I decided to run the bar myself. It's a bit more money, and if someone sexually harasses me I sexually harass them back or throw them out. My choice."

"Uh-huh."

My shift went until seven. Pepper explained that most days there was a little rush between five and seven as people got off their day jobs. The quietest time was from two to five. That's when I was supposed to restock. Just off the bar was a small storage room where the extra booze was kept. Everything I took out of there had to be written down on a clipboard. She kept a running inventory, which she double-checked every three months.

At eleven o'clock we opened the bar. Surprisingly, or at least surprisingly to me, there were a few people waiting for us to unlock the door. Pepper explained that a lot of the people who came in to V-Bar first thing in the morning had jobs where they worked all night. This was their 11 p.m., rather than their 11 a.m. Most of them would be gone by two o'clock, just as if she'd called last call.

Pepper introduced me to Bobby G., Tran and Connie. Without asking for orders, she started to build their drinks: Smirnov and Coke, house white on the rocks, and a mandarin vodka and cran.

"It's more important to learn people's drinks than their names," Pepper whispered to me as she poured. She had me put the drinks in front of them while she picked up the money they put down and cashed them out.

"I don't let people run tabs in the daytime. They tend to wander out, and when they wander back in the next day they try to say they paid. Honestly, I don't think they remember. It's safer to collect when the drinks are ordered."

Bobby G. and Tran spent most of their time sullenly staring at the two TVs that sat on shelves up by the ceiling. Each was tuned to a different iteration of ESPN. One played soccer, the other classic football games. Connie, though, was a talker. If I got within three feet of her, she'd start.

She didn't seem so bad. In fact, I kind of felt sorry for her. She worked the night shift at an all-night diner. In fact, she still wore her uniform, though on top of it she wore a cardigan with a sprinkling of sequins. She worked from midnight through eight in the morning. "They call it graveyard, but we get a good crowd. We're one of the only places in town open all night, so we get a decent rush after the bars close and then that blends right into the pre-work crowd. It's a better gig than you'd think."

Connie was in her mid-thirties and I figured she was lying about the job. It sounded dreadful. She wore a lot of perfume—one with too much lemon, I think—but when I'd set down her drinks, I could also smell pancakes and whatever it was she'd been drinking between the time she got off work and the time we opened. She'd probably been drop-dead gorgeous when she was younger, and had made the mistake of thinking she could get by forever on her looks. Now she looked worn and puffy from too much drinking.

Around one, Pepper sent me to lunch. "Normally you'll be alone, so you either need to bring your lunch or order in. You can eat behind the bar. Do you smoke?"

"No." I really was trying to quit. I hadn't had a cigarette in nearly three days. So it was sort of true. And if

I could pretend to be straight at work, I could pretend to be a nonsmoker.

"Good. I hate it when bartenders spend half their time out on the sidewalk. Do you drink?"

"Sometimes."

"The regulars are going to try to buy you drinks instead of tipping you. Not a great idea. You can drink if you want to, but if I come in here and find you shit-faced we'll have a problem."

I nodded. I really didn't plan to drink during the day. I had to leave myself something to do in the evening.

"Keep the comps to a minimum. If you think someone's new, you can comp them a drink. If your friends come in, comp them one drink the first time and then throw them a drink every other time they come in."

"Don't have a lot of friends."

"Well, now that you're a bartender you will." She lowered her voice. "Don't comp the regulars unless it's their birthday. And even then check their ID to make sure they're not lying. Otherwise they'll have six birthdays a year. Bottom line, they're going to try to squeeze drinks out of you at every opportunity. Don't let them con you."

She turned and smiled at the regulars as though she'd just been whispering sweet nothings about them.

"Go have lunch. There's a Mexican place three doors down. You should try it, it's pretty good."

I took her advice, and half an hour later I'd finished three street tacos and an iced tea. I took four ibuprofen, and tried to keep my foot elevated on the chair across from me through the whole lunch hour. Before I went back down to V-Bar, I called Carlos.

"Oh my Gawd, Carlotta, I'm in the closet!"

"Lynette, that's what pretending to be straight is. Didn't you know?"

"But I've never really been in the closet. I didn't even think I *could* be in the closet."

"Straight people always think someone's straight until you tell them. You could have a dick in your mouth and a butt plug up your ass, and a straight person would say, 'Do you have a girlfriend?'"

"No one's asked me that yet."

"When they do, tell them your heart is broken. That way you don't have to produce a girl for months."

"Can I do this for months?"

"Of course you can, you're the Meryl Streep of closet cases."

"Do I *want* to do this for months?"

###

I didn't stay at Lionel's long after I said that I liked him anyway. He didn't want to talk about it anymore and it didn't seem like he wanted to talk about anything else, so I left. Besides, sometimes it's better if I think about things for a while. I'm not always that quick. I mean, I kinda didn't get what the big deal was, and if I was going to apologize for it the right way I needed time to figure it out.

When I got home I checked my email. I'd been avoiding it since I sent out my resignation from the team. I'd also been avoiding my voicemail or even thinking about it. That's why I didn't tell Lionel I'd quit the team, because I didn't want to think about it. Plus, I didn't want him to feel guilty.

I opened my inbox and was kind of surprised there was only one email. I guess I shouldn't have been, though. The one and only email I got was from Chuckie.

It said, "Fuck you." He'd hit reply all. No one had the guts to say anything after that. Of course, they could have sent me an email meant just for me. They didn't have to hit reply all. Oh well. Crap.

I did have a voicemail from Fetch that had come in while I was at work on Monday a couple of hours after I'd sent the email.

"Hey dude, you working tomorrow? I think you sometimes have Tuesdays off. Let me know. Tim and I were thinking we could have lunch or something. Call me back."

I did have the day off, though I was surprised Fetch figured out my schedule. I worked a weird, four days on two days off schedule that I ended up having to trade around so I could get every Sunday off. I called Fetch and set a time to have lunch with the two of them at Nectar, a place with terrible food but a nice garden courtyard.

Tim and Fetch were already there when I arrived. They had a pitcher of mimosas on the table. Tim worked at home doing some kind of computer thing and Fetch managed a bookstore—though he said he hated reading—and usually worked during the week.

"Why are you off today?" I asked, when I sat down.

"Called in sick." Which gave me some idea that this was important.

After the waiter brought me a glass so I could share in the mimosas, we ordered. Hamburgers all around—really the only thing at Nectar that was decent. Then Tim got down to business. "So you quit the team but you're still going to play, right?"

"You're signing up as a free agent, right?" Fetch echoed.

"I haven't thought about it much."

It was a casual league, which meant that some Sundays not many people showed up. You had to have nine players to field a team. Free agents were around to keep a team from having to forfeit. I really hadn't thought about it, but now that Fetch and Tim mentioned it, I might do it.

"Do you think Chuckie will try to trash me with the other captains if I sign up to be a free agent?"

"Chuckie is an asshole," Tim said, surprising me. "The other teams don't have any reason to put up with him."

"So it doesn't matter what he says about you," Fetch said. "And, yeah, he's an asshole."

"Why *do* we put up with him?" I asked. I had some idea, of course. Chuckie was really social. He knew everyone. He was involved in a bunch of charities. Gave enormous parties. He was popular. And if you didn't get to know him, he was really likeable.

"I think it's Bob," Fetch said.

Tim continued, "Chuckie makes a big deal about Bob liking him, so the guys think no Chuckie, no sponsor for the team."

"Didn't Lionel say something about Bob not really liking him?" I asked.

"Yeah, but that's probably bullshit," Fetch said. "I mean, I don't think Lionel should have gotten fired, but that doesn't mean he didn't do anything wrong."

"He didn't do anything wrong. Chuckie called him a name. Just because he's a waiter doesn't mean he has to put up with that kinda thing."

"Lionel does provoke people, though," Tim said. "Look at what happened on Sunday."

"You mean when Chuckie shoved Lionel and he sprained his ankle."

"Well...look at the shoes he was wearing," Fetch said.

"Wait, are you friends with Lionel?" Tim asked.

"Yeah, kind of," I said. Part of me was tempted to say

no and I really hated that part of me.

"Are you more than friends?"

"Yeah."

They both said, "Oh."

I could tell they were trying to figure out if that changed things at all, so I decided to move on. "Look, life would be a lot easier if Chuckie weren't the asshole in all of this. But he is. And if you guys want to keep putting up with him, that's your business."

"No, we already decided to feel out the rest of the team about getting rid of him."

"We did?" Fetch asked.

"Yes, we did."

"Oh. Okay. I guess we did."

They didn't say anything for a minute. The waiter brought our hamburgers and we waited while he spread them out in front of us. I was about to bite into my burger when Fetch asked, "So, is that your type? Girly boys?"

"No. I mean, I'm not sure I have a type."

"Mmmmmhhhhhhmmm...We've heard that one before."

CHAPTER FIFTEEN

After my first full day at V-Bar, I wasn't sure whether to be proud of myself or suicidal. I was passing for straight, something I'd never thought I could do. Before she left, Connie even asked if I had a girlfriend. I just shook my head and mumbled, "Dating sucks." On the other hand, I was passing as straight so I was denying the person I'd been all my life. I felt like I was putting more value on the fake me than I gave the real me, and that felt very, very wrong.

I'd barely gotten onto the sidewalk outside V-Bar when I heard honking. I looked around and there was Dog in his truck. I limped over. The window on the passenger side rolled down and he said, "Get in."

I didn't.

"I gave you my phone number. You could have called me."

"I wanted to see you. And I didn't want you walking home. How's your ankle?"

"Sore. I wasn't going to walk home. I was going to take the bus."

"Okay. Do you want to take the bus?"

The odds of being in a knife fight were much lower

in Dog's truck. "No, I suppose not."

"Great. Get in."

I climbed into the truck, being careful not to jostle my ankle too much. I'd checked it in the men's room. It was swollen and a tad chartreuse after standing on it all day. I was going to have to spend the whole night with my foot in the air.

"How was your first day at work?"

"There are a few words I have to say before I spontaneously combust: Oh my Gawd! Fabulous! Sweetheart, darling, lovey. Well excuse the fuck out of me. You go girl! Lady Gaga, Brittany, Beyoncé, beotch. Sashay away."

He gave me the side eye. "Did you get that out of your system?"

"I've spent the whole day trying to only say 'yup,' 'nope' and 'I hear ya, man.' It was exhausting. I don't know how you do it."

"I say more than three things."

"You understand what I'm saying, though."

He shrugged. "I just do what comes naturally."

"Well, it's not natural to me, that's for sure. Ugh, and straight people are really boring."

"You may not find a good sampling working the dayshift at V-Bar."

"No you're right. I'm sure the *interesting* straight people, the bikers and the meth heads, come out at night."

He didn't outright laugh at that but he did kind of smirk. I liked that. Making him smirk. Making him outright laugh would be even better, but I'd settle for what I could get. I knew I should still be angry at him, but I was having a hard time of it. What he said mattered. But I also knew he hadn't meant anything bad by what he—

"So, I was thinking about what I said..."

Excellent. He was going to apologize and that whole thing would be over and I could concentrate on making him laugh. Actually, I wanted to concentrate on making him laugh while he was nak—

"...and I want to say that I like you *anyway*."

"Wait. That's the same thing you said before." Seriously? He was doubling down?

"It is."

"So you're sticking with that."

"I am."

"You don't see that it's a little insulting?"

"If you asked me a month ago if I wanted to hook up with someone as femme as you are, I would have said no. I didn't. But I did hook up with you. And what I found out is that I like you. I like you a lot."

"Anyway."

"Yes, anyway. Look, you know Fetch and Tim. Well, Fetch only goes out with Latino guys and Tim only goes out with Asian guys. If you spend five minutes with the two of them, you can figure out that they should be going out with each other, but neither one of them can see past what they think they like."

"So I'm not your type, but you like me."

"Yes. Am I your type? Do you always go out with bears?"

"You're more a cub actually. Bears are usually fa— heavier. You're husky."

"Are cubs your type?"

They weren't, actually, but I didn't want to admit it. I liked him and I guess I liked him in spite of the fact that he wasn't exactly my type. Actually, if I'm honest, my type had always been "willing," and certainly Dog had been that the night we hooked up. But I also didn't want to tell him that. Instead, I said, "I've always had a soft spot for baby animals—cubs, kittens, puppies."

The look on his face told me that he knew I was avoiding capitulation, and he didn't mind. And that was kind of interesting. He didn't have to make me wrong for him to be right. I couldn't remember another time where I'd fought with someone and it was okay to be right and wrong at the same time. I wondered what that meant?

"Should we get a pizza or something?" I asked.

"I promised I'd go over to my sister's. She wants to meet you, by the way."

"Oh my Gawd! How on earth does she even know about me?"

"I quit the Birdmen. I had her help me with my resignation email. She's better with words than I am."

"And my name came up?"

"It is kind of about you."

"Wait. You gave up softball for me?"

"Not exactly. I'm going to be what's called a free agent for a while. I'll play with any team that is short on players."

That didn't make a lot of sense. I mean, wasn't one of the basics of being good at sports that you actually had to show up? I decided to ignore his explanation completely, and said, again, with a ridiculous amount of pleasure, "You gave up softball for me."

###

We sat in front of Lionel's apartment, double-parked, making out for a good twenty minutes. It wasn't what you'd call comfortable. I'd gotten the 40/20/40 seats, so there wasn't a console in the way, but I did make Lionel elevate his foot on the dashboard, which kinda put him in my lap so I had to bend over to kiss him. By the time we were finished we each had a good case of razor burn.

His lips and the skin around them were all pink, and that was kind of appealing so I just wanted to keep kissing him.

"What's this?" I asked, pointing at a small scar that crossed his upper lip.

"You can see that?" he said, sounding surprised.

"When I'm this close."

"No biggie. I got into a fight with a couple of guys when I was in ninth grade."

It took me a moment to translate that. I imagined fifteen-year-old Lionel with flitty hands and an attitude picking a fight with a couple of guys. Nope, that didn't work. A couple of assholes ganging up on him made more sense.

"I'm sorry. I'm sorry that happened to you."

He shrugged and said, "Shit happens."

I kissed his scar and kept kissing him. A minute or so later, he pushed me away. "Either you stop or you come inside."

I was tempted to blow off my sister, but she'd said she had a letter from my dad and that was progress. I should at least go find out what it said. I wasn't expecting it to be easy to read, but the fact that he'd written anything at all was a good sign. Or at least I hoped it was.

"All right. I'm going."

He sat up, carefully lifting his leg off the dash. "Call me. I mean, if you want to."

"I'll call you," I promised. Then I watched him get out of the truck and hobble into his apartment complex. Just before he went in he turned and waved at me.

Twenty minutes later, I pulled into my sister's driveway. Arthur opened the door. "She's in the kitchen with some W-I-N-E. Make sure she drinks the whole bottle. She's easier to deal with when she's D-R-U-N-K."

I nodded, said, "Nice to see you, Arthur," then

hurried though the house before he could spell anything else. When I got into the kitchen, Maddy was sitting next to an open bottle of red wine. The minute she saw me she said, "I'm sorry. I did not want to give this to you, but Dad made me."

I almost asked, *Are you twelve?* but the distressed look on her face made me want to be nice to her. She held out a single piece of paper. I took it and glanced at it. There wasn't much on it.

"The isn't a letter. It's a note."

"He called it a letter. I was too traumatized to argue."

I read the note:

Doug—

I've been thinking this through and I want to ask you a question. And I want you to answer honestly. You went through a bad patch where you drank too much and got into some trouble. Is this like that? Is this just a bad patch? Think about it.

Your father

"Oh, that's nice," I said. "He thinks being gay is like drinking too much. Wow."

Maddy shrugged and said, "I'm sorry. I'd offer you a beer, but that would make me an enabler."

I ignored her and went over to her fridge and got out a PBR. "You better watch out. If you finish that whole bottle, you'll turn lesbian."

She smiled at me. "Oh, Arthur would like that. He'd want to watch."

"Yeah, I don't think lesbians are big on having straight guys watch. You know?"

"You're probably right. If I drink half the bottle, will I be bi?"

That made us laugh.

"Did Mom have anything to say about this? I assume you've talked to her."

"She just keeps saying she's working on him. I don't know what that means, though, other than they're quoting the Bible at each other a lot."

"Oh crap."

"He keeps quoting the Old Testament; she keeps quoting the New. He wants to call his new minister to talk to you; she wants to call the minister from our old church."

"The one they stopped going to because it's too liberal?"

"That's the one. They've each accused the other of stacking the deck a couple of times."

"Poor mom. Poor both of them."

"I don't feel sorry for them. It's not the Dark Ages. It's not like the issue isn't on the news all the time." Maddy finished her glass of wine and poured another.

"They never thought it had anything to do with them."

"I don't know how they can think that. Ever since I had kids, everything has to do with me as a parent. What kind of world is it going to be for them? Is the world even going to be there when they grow up? Who are they going to be?"

"You might be biting off more than you can chew."

She gasped a little. "Oh shit. I just realized something. My children have a gay uncle. That's amazing."

"Why is that amazing?"

"Because if one of them happens to be gay, they'll have someone to help them through it."

"You could help them through it."

"But you have insight. You know all the secrets."

"There are no secrets. We don't meet at midnight and practice ancient rituals."

"Um, excuse me, what do you think a gay bar is?"

CHAPTER SIXTEEN

My second day working at V-Bar was pretty much like the first, except Pepper left for most of it. She let me in and then sat at a table doing some bookkeeping while I set up. When I was done, she checked my work, made a few corrections, but still gave me a key so she could start sleeping in again.

"I'm going home to take a nap. I'll be back around five. If you have any problems, you can call me. I won't answer the phone, but you can call me."

"Okay," I said, realizing this was the straight guy way of expressing assurance, fear, hope, optimism and doubt. All in one word. I was in a pretty good mood. I felt confident in my newly acquired bartending skills, my ankle was improving and I could almost stand on it, and I had plans with Dog that evening.

Since dinner out had been kind of a bust and Dog's cooking for me hadn't turned out much better, we decided on pizza and a DVD. I tried to think about which of my DVDs I liked least so that we didn't have to watch the whole thing. I hoped we'd be in bed having sex before the pizza had time to get cold.

At eleven, I let the regulars in: Connie, Tran and

Bobby G. Within the hour, two more showed up. New to me but not to the other regulars. They were a young guy named John Michael, who had a tremor, and an older woman named Barb. As I kept them in drinks they asked the occasional question. After answering a few of them, Where was I from? Where'd I go school? What was my last job? I realized I was putting together an alternate identity. A me who was kind of me but not exactly.

I told them which suburb I'd grown up in, but I didn't get too specific about exactly where. I told them which high school I went to, but didn't talk about not finishing. In fact, I repeated my resume lie about doing a year at community college, just because I could. I told them my last job was on one of the cruise ships, since I didn't think any of them could afford to travel. That was different from my fake resume, but I didn't think Pepper had even checked, so what the heck.

I kept trying to turn the conversation around to them, but they all knew one another so that didn't hold their interest. Each time one of them answered a question about themselves, the others interrupted and turned the conversation back to me.

"You have a girlfriend?" Barb asked.

"He's broken-hearted," Connie said. It wasn't exactly what I'd told her, but it worked. I tried to look sad. Or at least as sad as a straight guy would look—which I guess wasn't very.

"Tell us about it," Barb insisted.

Ah, a fork in the road. I could refuse entirely. I could tell a story similar to my own life and just change the pronouns, which might be easier to remember. Or, I could just make up the most outrageous story I could think of.

"Lesbian. Dumped me for a chick with a Harley."

"Harleys are cool," said Tran.

"So are lesbians," said John Michael.

"You are both heartless bastards. Can't you see he's crushed," Connie said. "He's sensitive."

I tried looking sad again, but I think it came out angry. That's when I realized the only emotion straight guys were really comfortable showing was anger. That was sad—not to mention exhausting.

I had to take a piss, so I got everyone another round of drinks. This was a trick Pepper told me about. "Make sure everyone's got a fresh drink before you hit the can. That way they can't jump behind the bar and pour their own refill."

While I was in the bathroom I made a mental list of who I was becoming at V-Bar. Leo, broken-hearted, lesbian ex-girlfriend, local, a little college, sensitive. If it got too much more elaborate, I was going to have to write things down. When I walked out of the men's room, I found Barb and Connie rolling around on the floor tearing at each other's hair.

Yes, I wanted to scream, *CAT FIGHT!* but instead, I said, "Hey, ladies? Could you stop that?" Of course, they were screaming like banshees so they couldn't hear me.

"Ladies. I'm going to have to call the police."

Bobby G., Tran and John Michael stood over them egging them on. Mostly with "Atta girls" and "Get hers" so they could claim to be rooting for whichever woman won and was willing to buy them drinks.

"Ladies!" I tried a little more forcefully. Barb had her thumb up Connie's nose and I had to do something before she ripped her nostril a la *Chinatown* so I screamed, "BITCHES, PLEASE!"

That got their attention. They looked up at me from the floor. I was afraid for a moment that I'd completely blown it. So I looked at them sullenly and said, "Hey. Cut the shit."

They scrambled off the floor. Second day on the job and I had my first dilemma. I wanted to throw them both out and tell them to never come back, but they were regulars.

"I'm gonna give you one more chance. Behave or get out."

They looked sheepish. Though each probably wanted the other thrown out for good, neither wanted it to happen to them.

"Don't you want to know whose fault it was?" Connie asked.

"No, I don't," I said. If I knew whose fault it was I'd have to throw one of them out, and I didn't want to do that. "Does this happen a lot?"

The two women shook their head no, while the men in the bar nodded their heads yes. *Great*, I thought, *bartender and referee*. My horizons were expanding.

My cell phone, which I'd left near the cash register, rang. I picked it up as I watched Connie and Barb sit back down at the bar. I did kind of want to know what had caused the fight. Was it over a man? Was it over one of the men at the bar? That was hard for me to imagine, but then I rarely understood women's taste in men. In fact, how and why straight people hooked up was a complete mystery.

Dog was on the phone sounding contrite. "I'm sorry, but I think I have to cancel tonight. I have to go over to my parents. I think my dad might be coming around."

###

I arrived at my parents' house about seven, just as I was told to. My sister's Odyssey was parked on the street. There was a green Ford Edge I didn't recognize in the driveway, which should have told me something was up.

My mom answered the door, still dressed in pink scrubs, her face red. At first, I wasn't sure if she was angry or having a hot flash. When she hissed, "Leave this to me," under her breath, I knew it was anger. She led me back to the family room where my dad was sitting on the overly large sectional next to a neatly dressed guy in his early thirties. My sister was huddled around the corner of the sectional, glaring at them.

"Hey, Dad, what's going on?" I asked.

"It's a kidnapping, Dougie. Run for your life," Maddy blurted.

My mother played hostess. "Would anyone like a cup of coffee? Tea? I have several kinds of soda—"

"I'd like a glass of wine," Maddy said.

"Yes dear, you've mentioned that. Repeatedly. Anyone else?"

"I'll have a cup of tea," the stranger said.

"This is Hector Arcana," my dad said. "He's with Gay Anon and he's here to tell you about their program and the remarkable success they have."

"Gay Anon?" I said, dumbly.

"It's a weird name, right?" Maddy said. "It makes me think of Shakespeare. Like, 'I will be gay, anon.'"

"It's short for Anonymous," Hector said. "Our program is based on highly successful twelve-step programs. The only thing Doug needs to do is want to change."

"Dad, this really isn't okay," I said.

"I'm only asking for an hour of your time. I raised you, gave you everything it was in my power to give, I think you can give me an hour."

That sounded reasonable enough that I couldn't find a way to say no, even though I wanted to. I sat down uncomfortably on the sectional.

Hector smiled in a friendly but creepy way. "By the

time I was twenty-five I'd had sex with nearly five thousand men."

My dad's eyes got really big and he looked at me for the first time since I'd walked in. He was thinking I was twenty-six so that meant...

"I was miserable, desperate, hopeless—"

I had to interrupt him. "Hold on a minute. We need to do some math. There are three hundred and sixty five days a year. One guy a day for ten years would only be three thousand six hundred and fifty. So even if you started when you were fifteen and even if you were a prostitute...you'd have to be a really, really popular one who never, ever took a day off—"

"I didn't keep a scorecard. It's an estimate." Hector scowled at me.

"I think you've over estimated by a lot and you're scaring the crap out of my dad."

"I'm fine, Dougie. If I need to subject myself to the tragic details of your life in order to help you get bet—"

"Ten. Ten, Dad. Ten guys. Three girls. Okay?" Information I did not ever want to give my dad, but I knew he was imaging gigantic crowd scenes at that particular moment.

"Ten? Are you kidding?" Maddy practically screamed. "I screwed thirty-two guys before Arthur. And three after. You're such a lightweight."

"Madison! You're here to help. That is not helping." There was sweat on my father's forehead and he looked pale.

"We really shouldn't get tied up in numbers," Hector continued. "The important part of my story is that I was miserable, desperate, hopeless. The shame was crushing. I couldn't live with it. I don't know what would have happened to me if I hadn't found Gay Anon." Then he looked at me intently. "Doug, the first thing I want you to understand is that this is not entirely your fault." He glanced at my dad uncomfortably and then said, "With all due respect, homosexuality is the result of an overbearing mother and an absent father."

"HA!" My sister guffawed. "We've got you there. My mom worked, she was never around enough to be overbearing. And my dad did everything with Dougie. Which, by the way Dad, might explain the thirty—"

"Madison! I'm going to ask you to leave if you don't stop interrupting."

Just then, my mom came back with two mugs of tea. She handed one to Hector. "I wasn't sure, but you seemed like a two sugars and a splash of cream kind of guy." Somehow she managed to make that sound like an insult.

"What did I miss?" she asked.

"You're overbearing," Maddy said. "I defended you by explaining we were latch-key kids."

"Well, as long as I take all the blame I'm fine with it." She handed Maddy the second cup of tea.

"This is tea. I asked for wine."

"You can be an alcoholic when your children are grown," my mom said in her sweetest do-as-I-say-voice.

"That's sixteen years."

"We've gotten off track. Hector is giving us his valuable time to share his experience recovering from the horrors of homosexuality," my dad said. There must have been a brochure or website somewhere where he'd read that. I didn't think he'd come up with 'horrors of homosexuality' on his own.

"Oh yes, dear," my mother said. "Let's discuss the *horrors* of homosexuality."

"Hector just explained he's had sex with five thousand men."

"Really? Well that is horrible." My mother smiled when she said it.

"Finally," my dad said. "Finally, one of you is willing to listen."

"Wilt Chamberlain. Do you remember, dear? You read his biography. Now, you told me he claimed to have slept with twenty thousand women. Would you call that the horrors of heterosexuality or the horrors of basketball?"

My father seethed. I almost felt sorry for him.

"Look," Hector said. "Doug, the important thing you need to know is that there's help if you want it. Like other twelve-step programs, the first step is recognizing you have a problem, and what I'm picking up on is that you're not ready to take that step. So when you are ready to take that step remember that Gay Anon is here for you."

The doorbell rang.

"I'll get it," my mom said, jumping up.

"Who is that?" my dad asked.

No one answered him. I realized this might be an opportunity to put to an end to this, so I said to Hector, "Thanks for coming by. I appreciate the information." I actually didn't, but he was more likely to leave if I did. "At the moment, though, the only real problem I have is my family."

"I'm not a problem," Maddy insisted. "Mom's not a problem."

My mom walked back into the room in time to hear Maddy. "Of course I'm a problem. Mothers are always a problem."

There was a very short man in his fifties standing next to her. She introduced him, "This is Chaplain Davis. I work with him at the hospital."

"Dora, what are you doing?" my dad asked.

"He has a different opinion than the gentleman you've brought."

"We don't need other opinions."

"If you can have surprise guests, so can I. Have a seat, chaplain."

Hector stood up. "I should really go."

"You have a few more minutes, don't you?" my mom said, then turned to her chaplain. "This is Hector, he's had sex with five thousand men."

"Ah," said Chaplain Davis. "It's a shame he has to leave. But then it is still happy hour at The Bird."

Hector was at least familiar enough with The Bird to be offended. "Actually, my wife is waiting for me. But I think she'd want me to stay." Hector plunked back down.

Then they went at it for an hour and a half. At one point, my mom brought out chips and dip. Chaplain Davis clearly had the more logical arguments, something my dad seemed increasingly unhappy about. Either that or he had indigestion.

After a while, I stopped paying attention and started thinking about how lucky I was. I was a grown up. I didn't have to stay. I could walk out at any time. If I'd come out when I was a teenager, I might have had to go through the same kind of thing. And if my mom hadn't been supportive... If both my parents were thinking like my dad, then I'd have been stuck. Working all of the twelve steps with Hector.

CHAPTER SEVENTEEN

It was nearly midnight and I was curled up in bed eating my absolutely favorite pizza in the whole world, Hawaiian double pineapple. After my first bite I had a startling revelation. I was twenty-three and the most significant relationship in my life was with pizza. Seriously, I spent more time with pizza than any one person. I had pizza several times a week. Other than keeping it warm, a relationship with pizza was very low maintenance. And it was certainly more satisfying than most of the men I'd dated. *Oh my Gawd!* I'd discovered a new sexuality. I was a pizza-sexual. Well, maybe not, I didn't actually want to have sex with pizza. Okay, maybe a little oral, but I considered myself mostly pizza-romantic. Still, that meant I was going to have to come out to people all over again.

I was on my third slice and still giggling about being a pizza-sexual when Dog called.

"It sounds awful," I said after he told me what had happened at his parents.

"It was. But listen, I was wondering, did you ever have anything like that happen to you?"

"Oh, um..." I tried to think. "You know I have a

vague memory of my dad bringing a minister home once. He left us alone in my room and the guy put his hand on my knee. I thought he was making a pass. After that, my dad tried playing catch with me in the backyard a couple of times. That was a disaster."

"I just, I sort of had this moment where I realized that life has been easier for me, you know, since people can't always figure out I'm gay."

"Easier than it's been for me, is that what you mean?"

"Yeah, I mean...were you ever in the closet?"

The answer was no, of course, but I hated that he was assuming that I couldn't—"I'm in the closet right now. At work."

"Oh yeah, I know that." He waited for a moment, then asked, "So you actually told them you're straight."

"Not in so many words. I let them assume." Actually, I did more than that. I told them my ex-girlfriend left me for a lesbian.

"How do you feel about that?" Dog asked.

"What do you mean, how do I feel about it? I feel like I'm paying my rent. I don't think you get to criticize, you didn't come out to your parents until a few days ago."

"My dad has a heart condition, I thought—"

"But you were wrong. He hasn't had a heart attack and he hasn't died. Maybe you were taking the easy way out?"

Why was I being mean to him? I wondered. Probably because I didn't want to think too closely about what I was doing myself. And thinking that made me think a little harder. Why was what I was doing okay? Did I really want to lie about myself? Nothing would ever get better if I kept lying, now would it? Fortunately, no one had said anything nasty about gay people in the two days

I'd worked at V-Bar, but I had to assume someone eventually would. And what would I do when that happened? Would I let them get away with it?

"Maybe I *was* taking the easy way out," Dog said.

"What?" I was too busy thinking to follow the conversation.

"I said, maybe I was taking the easy way out."

"Oh Gawd, I'm sorry. You know, how you came out to your parents is your business and I shouldn't have said that."

"It's okay. I can take it," he said, and then a moment later asked, "What are you wearing?"

"Seriously?"

"Yeah, seriously, what are you wearing?"

I had on a pair of flannel pajama bottoms, a T-shirt that said, "I'm so GAY I can't even think STRAIGHT" and several pizza stains. None of which were even remotely sexy.

"I'm wearing a navy blue jock strap and a crisp white wife beater that shrunk in the laundry. It barely covers my belly button."

He laughed. "No you're not."

"I could be."

"What are you really wearing?"

"Flannel pajama bottoms."

"Mmmmm, sexy."

"You're teasing me."

"I like flannel. Pull them down a little."

"You want to have phone sex?"

"Yeah, why not?"

"Darling, you know, we could cam." As soon as I said it I regretted it. If we cammed I'd have to take a shower and fix my hair and actually dig out that jockstrap which I thought was in the bottom drawer of my dresser but might not actually be.

"Let's do it old school. That way we don't have to spend half the time trying to find a good angle."

"Oh my, you know me too well."

"Pull your pajama bottoms down."

"All right," I pulled them down part way.

"I remember your ass, how round it is."

"From the night we met? I thought you didn't remember."

"I remember the next morning very well."

"What are you wearing?" I asked. Tit for tat, after all.

"Boxer briefs. That's all."

I thought about him almost naked; his hairy belly, his thick thighs. I slipped my hand in my pajama bottoms. "Leave them on. I want you to rub your dick through them."

"Okay."

"Are you rubbing it?"

"I am."

"Good boy. Slip your hand in and grab your cock by the base." I'd jumped ahead and done that to myself. "Have you got it?"

"Uh-huh."

I pushed my pajama bottoms all the way down. My prick was hard and oozing a tad.

"What do you want me to do now?" Dog asked.

"Pump it. Move your fist up and down. Slowly. And squeeze."

I shut my eyes and imagined him. His hand down his boxers, pumping his dick. His big body tensing. A surprised look in his warm brown eyes as a damp spot spread across the front of his boxer briefs. And then I clenched, spasmed, spurted up and across my chest, gasped a little and almost said, *Holy shit.*

I listened to him breathing heavily. I'd had no idea I was about to come. I was kind of embarrassed. It hadn't taken any time at all. I didn't want Dog to think I had a "problem." I mean, I didn't. I was just kind of into him and thinking about...wow, I was really into him. I didn't know if it was a good idea for him to know that. Or to know exactly how—

"Are you not feeling this?" he asked.

"Oh. Um. You know, it is kind of silly."

"It is, you're right."

"I mean, you're only ten minutes away..."

"I know. I'm sorry. Bad night. We need to have sex again, though. How long has it been?"

"Decades," I said.

"Two weeks, I think."

"Feels like decades."

After I hung up, I fell asleep. Didn't even bother to change my underwear, which now had a big cum stain all over the front. I couldn't believe Lionel did that to me. We were just talking and then boom. I really wanted to get the rest of my life under control so I could spend some time with him. A lot of time. In bed.

The next morning, I was driving to work when Fletch and Tim conference-called me. I hit the button on the steering wheel and said hello to them both.

"Something going on?" I asked.

"A lot," Tim said.

"A whole lot," Fetch upped the ante.

"Like what?"

"We've been talking to the team."

"Feeling them out about Chuckie."

"No one likes him."

"Okay, that's not a surprise," I said.

"But—"

"Yeah, but—"

"But what?"

"We think Chuckie knows."

"Yeah, he might be onto us."

"Knows what? Onto what?" I asked.

"That the team wants you back."

"And that we want you to be captain."

"Oh. Okay." This was news to me. "Um, well how do you know he knows that?"

"Because he's selling Donny Talbert's condo. For a reduced commission," Tim said. Donny played center field.

"And he hired Wendell Winslow to redo his website," Fetch added. Wendell was third base.

"Those could just be good business decisions."

"Could be."

"Maybe."

"Either way though, Donny and Wendell aren't going to make a move against him now, that's what you're saying?"

"They might still. If Bob does."

"If Bob wants Chuckie gone, everyone will go along."

"You know, guys…I'm fine going free agent. I don't need to be team captain. Okay?"

"Right."

"Oh yeah."

They continued. "So what we need to do is sit Bob down and lay everything out."

"Make sure he understands how the team feels."

"We've set up a meeting for tonight."

"At The Bird. Eight o'clock."

"Okay. Let me know how that goes," I said.

"Oh, no, you're coming with us. Someone needs to teach Chuckie a lesson."

"And that someone is you."

Reluctantly, I agreed to meet with Bob and then hung up.

Crap, I thought, *how was I going to convince Bob to dump Chuckie?* I'd never thought of myself as the persuasive type. I had no idea why Fetch and Tim thought I could convince anyone of anything. Then it hit me. My email. The one Maddy wrote. They thought I was the kind of person who said things like 'intolerable situation' and 'coerce.' Crap. I wondered if they'd mind if Maddy went to meet with Bob?

That's what I was thinking about when I got off the elevator on the fifth floor. I turned toward Cardiac Testing and ran right into my father.

"Dad? What are you doing here? Is Mom okay?"

"Your mother is a pain in the ass."

"But she's healthy?"

"Very."

"Good," I relaxed, then wondered again what he was doing there. I had a bad feeling it wasn't going to be good.

"I've found a therapist I want you to talk to," he said, with too much concern in his voice.

"Dad, maybe *you* should see a therapist."

"Well, yes, after you've worked with this gentleman for a time he'll be inviting your mother and I to come in for a session with you. I've explained that your mother may be resist—"

"I mean, you should see a therapist for you. You're having trouble accepting that I'm gay."

"Accept it? You're talking as though I'm the one who needs to change."

"Dad, you are," I said as gently as I could. And then I walked away.

CHAPTER EIGHTEEN

My first completely unsupervised shift at V-Bar was Thursday. Everything went incredibly smoothly. I set up, opened the doors, the regulars rolled in, Connie and Barb managed not to get into a knock-down drag-out fight, and I had my lunch delivered—a veggie pizza bianca from a place down the street, major yummy. The morning crowd had their fill and staggered off. Around two o'clock, the only person in the bar was Connie. She'd had six mandarin vodka and crans, and was now shit-faced. After only three days of working as a bartender, I'd begun to think the terms we used for drunkenness actually corresponded well to various legal states.

Lit was what you called someone who'd blow about a .04 on a breathalyzer test. Feeling it but still legal. Toasted was just over the line into illegal. Shit-faced was so drunk it ought to be illegal for you to operate your own two feet. Connie was shit-faced.

I was afraid she'd order another drink, so I went into the storage room to restock. While I was trying to decipher Pepper's inventory sheet, I felt someone behind me. I turned to see Connie standing there.

"Connie, you shouldn't be back here."

"Lemme give you a blow job."

"No. Thank you." Why was I saying thank you? It wasn't like she'd offered me a napkin.

"Oh don't be like that, Leo. I can tell when a man is frustrated and you're a frustrated man."

"I'm fine, Connie."

"I will not take no for an answer."

"Um, that would be rape."

She laughed. "Ah, you're so funny! I'm not going to rape you! I'm gonna give you a blow job." She reached out to undo my belt. I slapped her hand away. "Ouch. That hurt."

"Connie, no means no."

"It does not. You're afraid of losing your job, aren't you? Don't worry I won't tell Pepper."

"Connie, no."

She came toward me again and I jumped back. It wasn't the idea of having sex with a woman that was so frightening. Well, all right, it was a tad frightening. But it was more Connie's need. She needed to give me a blow job. It meant something important to her, some sort of validation. If she sucked me off, she'd have value. Now, don't get me wrong, blow jobs are fun. But they're only fun if they're fun. You start layering on all sorts of meaning and they get to be a drag pretty quickly.

"Why are you acting like this?" she asked, getting on her knees.

"Get up. Off the floor."

She planted her hand dead center onto my crotch.

"AH! Oh my Gawd! Get off me you crazy bitch!" I swatted her hand off me, and without thinking briefly rested a hand near my throat.

She looked up at me, surprised. "Your voice changed."

Catching myself, I pulled it together. "Hey, if you go

back to the bar I'll comp you a drink, how about that?"

"You're a faggot, aren't you?"

Well, there was a dilemma. If I told Connie, then everyone at V-Bar would know I was gay, which was a problem. On the other hand, if I admitted the truth, then Connie would stop trying to force a blow job on me. That solved an immediate problem. I could deal with the bigger problem later.

"Yes, Connie, I'm gay. Go back to the bar. I'll make you a new drink and we'll have nice little talk." Surprisingly, she grabbed at my belt again.

"Hey, knock it off."

"You're not going to be the first fag I've sucked off and you won't be the last."

I tried to imagine what kind of gay guy would let a drunk woman call him names and administer fellatio. I came up blank. It made a lot more sense that some straight guy faked being gay so she could feel like she'd made a conquest. Of course, it didn't matter. I had to find a way to get her off me.

"Connie, you don't need to demean yourself like this."

"I'm not demeaning myself. I'm having a good time."

"You're on your knees in sleazy bar trying to have sex with someone who doesn't want you. That's not a good time. That's hitting bottom. It's time to take a good long look at your life."

Finally, she stood up. "Jesus Christ. You could have just said no. You didn't have to fucking attack me."

I was sure I'd said no repeatedly, but decided not to argue the point. Maybe I was the one who needed to take a good long look at his life. Working with really drunk people wasn't turning out as well as I'd hoped. In fact, why I'd ever thought it would turn out well was now completely escaping me. Of course, I realized I might not have to work with extremely drunk people for very much longer. Connie would very likely tell everyone in the bar, including Pepper, that I was gay.

That would have been just fine with me, except I was making better money at V-Bar than I'd ever made before. And, I didn't have to work nights. And, I hated looking for jobs. Of course, I was pretty sure it was illegal in California to fire someone for being gay. But, it was also legal to fire someone without giving them a reason. So as long as Pepper never said, "I heard you're gay so I'm firing you," she was probably okay.

"Are you going to tell everyone I'm gay?" I asked Connie.

She studied me, probably calculating what she might be able to get out of the situation. "Maybe. Maybe not."

"I won't tell anyone about what just happened."

"Oh, I don't care about that. Please."

"What *do* you care about?"

"My reputation. You have to tell everybody I sucked you off and it was the best you ever had."

###

Bob Grottoli was one of those people everyone talked about but no one ever saw. I've been going to The Bird regularly for about five years and I've seen him maybe twice. You know it's him because people tend to stop what they're doing and just stare in his direction. When I arrived, the place was pretty full, and Fetch and Tim were sitting at a table in the back.

It was Larry Lamour's night to host karaoke roulette. You signed up, and when it was your turn Lamour pulled a random song out of a glass bowl and you had to sing it. Lamour wore a Russian-style hat and a communist-red muumuu with an ermine collar. He looked even more ridiculous than usual, but he managed to pull in a crowd.

I sat down and said hey to the boys.

"You might want to go to the bar and get your own drink," Fetch said.

"Service has really declined without Lionel."

I looked over and saw the new waiter standing at a table of four guys, all much older and with very high incomes. He had a hand on the shoulder of one the guys and his other hand on his hip. He did not look like he was taking a drink order. Carlos, on the other hand, was fighting his way through the crowd with a full tray.

"Do you see Bob anywhere?"

"No"

Larry Lamour's voice came over the speaker system. "All right, Ladies and... Ladies, first up tonight we have... Tarquelle Washington. Did I say that right, sweetheart? Tar-kell?"

A tall, good-looking guy got up and shyly whispered something to Larry.

"Oh, sorry, Tar-kwell. Tarquelle will be singing..." Larry reached into a fishbowl full of slips of paper. "Doris Day's 'Secret Love'... Do you have a secret love Tarquelle?"

He shook his head emphatically, but his friends hooted and hollered that he did. Larry hit a few buttons on the karaoke machine and Tarquelle began stumbling through the song.

Carlos swooped by our table and took my order for a lite beer. Then he swooped away. And then, unexpectedly, Bob Grottoli was standing at our table. Around fifty, with a bad toupee and over-scrubbed skin, he was fidgety and nervous. The kind of person who didn't look right without a cigarette in hand, like he'd never learned to fit into a non-smoking world.

"You wanted to talk to me?" He looked around like we were in the middle of a drug deal. The three of us fell silent. I waited for Fetch or Tim, or Fetch *and* Tim to speak. They didn't. Kind of annoying since they'd set up the meeting. They could have at least gotten the ball rolling.

"Look," I said, not sure where I was going. "...A lot of the guys on the Birdmen are unhappy with Chuckie. They're thinking they'd like him to step down as captain."

"Didn't you quit the team?"

"I did. Because of the situation with Chuckie and Lionel."

"But the team wanted Lionel gone. So he's gone." Bob was clearly not enjoying the conversation.

"That's not a hundred percent true," Tim finally said.

"Yeah, Chuckie pressured people into emailing you."

Bob seemed to consider for a moment then said, "Well, we can't get rid of Chuckie."

"Why not?"

"How come?"

"Because he's Chuckie. Everyone loves Chuckie."

"No, everyone does not love Chuckie," I said. "Chuckie thinks that, but it's not true."

Bob looked confused. "Well, it's mostly true, isn't it?"

"Do you love Chuckie?" I asked.

"Sure," he said. It was not convincing.

"Do you really?"

"He can be...difficult. But he's been, well, sort of a friend."

"It's the 'sort of' that everyone's having a problem with," I pointed out.

"What do you want me to do about it?"

"Bob, you sponsor the team. You have a say."

"No, I don't think I do. I think it's up to the players."

"But they think it's up to you," Tim said.

"They do," agreed Fetch.

Tarquelle finished the Doris Day song and everyone in the bar clapped except the three of us.

"So you want me to 'fire' Chuckie from the team?" Bob asked to clarify.

"And rehire Lionel at the bar," I put in. Not that I thought Lionel wanted the job back, but he should at least have the option, right?

"Rehire—"

"The team doesn't really want him gone."

Panic filled his face. "Oh, did I say I fired him because of the team? I wasn't supposed to say that. Lionel's firing was completely unrelated to the requests I received from the team. And I can't, legally, discuss his firing. I mean, people come people go without any regard to, well, anything. It's all just, you know, a big coincidence."

"Then Lionel could be coincidentally rehired?" I suggested.

"Possibly. Maybe. I don't know. I'm not comfortable discussing any of this. I'll need to make a few calls."

Just then Larry announced, "Our next performer is...Chuckie Cooper. Come on up Chuckie."

The three of us looked in horror over to Larry Lamour just as he was joined by Chuckie. Larry reached into his fishbowl and pulled out a small slip of paper from which he read, "And the song you'll be singing Chuckie is... 'I Enjoy Being a Girl' from *Flower Drum Song*."

The bar erupted into laughter. Chuckie put his hand on Larry's mike and the two of them had an intense exchange. Finally, Larry said to us, "Apparently that's in the wrong key for Chuckie." Larry reached into the bowl a second time and came up with... "Oh, yes, this is a better key, Aerosmith's 'Dude Looks Like a Lady'!"

There was an even larger jolt of laughter and applause. Chuckie grabbed the slip of paper out of Larry's hand and read it. Then he shoved it back at Larry who made a big show of reading it again. "You know, I don't have my glasses, apparently this actually says 'Stairway to Heaven' by Led Zeppelin. My mistake."

Chuckie grabbed the mike away from Larry, who put in the correct numbers for the song. As Chuckie began to sing I turned back to the table and realized that Bob was gone.

And we didn't see him again that night.

CHAPTER NINETEEN

I desperately needed to make more friends. After work, I just had to talk to someone about what had happened with Connie, but Carlos was busy working and Dog was out with the team. That left me at loose ends. I could have gone home and spent the evening watching old movies, but I knew I wouldn't be able to concentrate. As I walked home I wondered briefly what Joan Crawford might do in my situation. It wasn't that hard to figure out. She'd have lied to get what she wanted in a heartbeat. Hell, she'd have let Connie blow her. Or, you know, whatever.

Too antsy to just go home, I decided to go to The Pub. I knew that Dog was down at The Bird, but I thought I should leave him alone with the team. I decided I'd text him later about possibly getting together. When I walked into The Pub I saw Linda Sue sitting on the far side of the bar. I went over and sat with her.

"Hello darling, stunning outfit," I said, politely. Actually, I meant stunning in the less flattering way, but didn't make a point of that. She wore a zebra-print wrap dress and a pair of low-heeled, silver sandals. I did say,

"Not to criticize, but a higher heal would do wonders for your calves."

"Bad knees. How's it going with you? You find a job yet?"

"I have. I'm working over at V-Bar."

"Oh yeah? My wife and I go in there sometimes. When we're slumming."

I wondered if I'd recognized her if she came in with her wife. Or his wife. I was pretty sure the cross-dresser rule was to match pronouns to clothing. So if Linda Sue came into V-Bar dressed as... oh, wait, I might not even be there.

"You'd better hurry if you want to see me there. My job is hanging by a thread."

"That happens to you a lot, doesn't it?"

"Yes. But it's rude to point out."

And then, over an Absolut and tonic, I told him the story of Connie and the blow job.

"You are in a pickle," she said when I was finished.

"So what should I do, Linda Sue?"

"I can't decide that for you. No one can."

That was not a very satisfying answer. On the one hand, I needed to have money to survive; on the other, I needed to be myself. Of course, being myself in the gutter seemed like a terrible idea. And that meant I was going to have to go to work in the morning and tell people that Connie gave terrific blow jobs. And then on Monday I'd start looking for a new situation. Again. Something where being myself was an actual option.

"How come you're not down at The Bird?" I asked Linda Sue.

"I walked in, but Chuckie's there. Not my favorite person."

"Nor mine."

I'd heard something about Chuckie not letting her

onto the Birdmen. Even though it was a gay softball team, Linda Sue wasn't exactly like most straight men. I could see them not wanting to be overrun by a lot of straight guys, but, come on, Linda Sue?

I finished my drink but decided not to have another. The Pub was usually stop two after people got bored at The Bird. I didn't want to be there when Chuckie got bored. I just wasn't in the mood. As I walked home, I texted Dog.

WHAT ARE YOU UP TO?

As I let myself into my apartment I got a text back. OUT WITH TIM AND FETCH TEXT YOU LATER. I showered—since I smelled like bourbon and maraschino cherries—threw on my PJs, tossed a frozen pizza into the oven and picked out the DVD *Bringing Up Baby* just so I could see Cary Grant in a nightgown saying, "I've just gone gay!" I made it to that point in the movie—and rewound that section to re-watch it about six times—but fell asleep long before the dinosaur collapsed.

In the morning there was a sweet text from Dog and an invitation to go to the movies. Which was great, because I was too freaked out by work to be angry at him for semi-blowing me off.

Fridays were a little busier than the rest of the week. People took extra vacation days or called in sick so they could drink for an extra day on the weekend. I was beginning to have the feeling that if I spent enough time as a bartender I might stop drinking completely. I was spending my days staring at a bar full of cautionary tales.

All the regulars were there and a few new ones. Connie, of course, sat dead center wearing a fluffy pink cardigan and awaiting her accolades. I knew I should do what she wanted, but I had no idea how to casually work her amazing fellatio skills into conversation. I mean, seriously, "Isn't the weather terrific and by the way

Connie gives great head" wasn't going to cut it.

After watching my every move for more than an hour, Connie couldn't stand it anymore and asked, "So...did anything interesting happen yesterday?"

Oh my Gawd! What did she think I was going to say? "Yea, Con, you gave me a great bj?" I mean, really. The only thing I could think of was, "Um, I don't kiss and tell." That was enough, though. Connie beamed like she'd just won the lottery. Tran and Bobby G. glanced at each other. Bobby G. said, "Oh shit. Not again."

"What does that mean?" I asked.

"Connie has a thing for bartenders."

"Oh."

"Maybe we should have told you to watch out," Tran said.

I blushed reflexively. Fortunately, even in the dim lighting they all saw it and it got a round of laughter. Suddenly, I had a brilliant idea. Breaking Pepper's rule against buying drinks for the regulars, I made a round of blow jobs for everyone at the bar. I set out seven shot glasses, poured Kahlua into the bottom of each, and topped that off with Baileys. When I got out the whipped cream everyone knew what I was doing and they sort of went crazy while I dolloped each shot.

I set the shots out in front of the regulars. Bobby G. reached for his. "Uh-huh. You've gotta do this the right way."

"Oh, no, I don't think so."

"Connie will demonstrate."

Pushing her stool back, she stood up in front of the bar. She moved the shot so it was right in front of her. She made a big show of putting her hands behind her back and then bent over the bar and opening her mouth carefully wrapped her lips around the shot glass. Quickly, she stood up, tossing her head back and downed the shot. That earned her a spattering of applause and a few catcalls.

The rest of the regulars refused at first, but eventually each of them put their hands behind their backs and did the shot. After all, it was alcohol and it was free. Connie was glowing like it was her wedding day.

I felt about three feet tall.

The first thing I did when I woke up was text Lionel an apology and invite him to go to the movies. My treat. Then I took an aspirin and drank a half-gallon of water. I had to get the softball thing under control. Once things calmed down there'd be a whole lot less drinking. To make matters worse, it was my early day. I had to be at work by eight, so I was up much earlier than I wanted to be.

When I got out of the shower, my cell phone was ringing. I dug it out of my jeans and saw that it was Maddy.

"I'm getting ready for work. Is it important?"

"What did you do to Dad?" she asked.

"What do you mean? I didn't do anything to him."

"He's acting really weird."

"And you just noticed? The whole intervention thing wasn't a tip off?" Using one hand I tried to struggle into a pair of boxers. It didn't go too well. I accidentally fell onto my bed.

"Weird in a different way. He called me and asked if I thought he was crazy."

I switched my phone over to speaker and lay it on the bed. "What did you say?"

"What happened? You sound like you're in a tunnel."

"I put you on speaker so I can get dressed."

"Ewwww...don't tell me you're naked."

"Don't call first thing in the morning. What did you say when Dad asked if you thought he was crazy?" I sat on the edge of the bed pulling on a pair of socks.

"Well, I said he wasn't crazy. I mean, I think he's wrong but that's different than crazy. Why did you call him crazy?"

"I didn't call him crazy. I said maybe he should see a therapist."

"That's not the kind of thing you say to Dad. He thinks only crazy people see therapists."

"Um, he told me I should see a therapist. He has one all picked out."

"Yeah, he mentioned that. I said I'd talk to you about it."

I had my scrubs part way on but stopped when she said that. "You did? So, you think I should go to a shrink and get fixed?"

"No, I don't think that. It's just...Dad's never asked for my help before."

"So I should go to therapy to fix your relationship with him?"

"Would you do that for me?"

"No."

"Okay," she said happily. "I didn't think you would. I told Dad I'd talk to you about it and we have, so I've done my daughterly duty. You don't mind if I tell him I tried really hard to be persuasive, do you?"

"As long as you don't actually try." I was fully dressed, so I picked up the phone and clicked it off speaker while I wandered around looking for my wallet, my keys, my sunglasses...

"Oh, don't worry," Maddy said. "I'm just trying to improve my relationship with Dad. And if I have to lie to do it, that's okay. Now, how's the boyfriend situation?"

"I don't have a boyfriend."

"The guy you quit the softball team for. Lionel."

It had been a real mistake to have her help me with that email. She now knew too much about my extracurricular activities. I was used to her not knowing much about that, and I liked it that way.

"Um, we kinda have a date tonight." I mean, I'd invited him. I hoped he'd say yes.

"What are you going to do?"

"I'm going to take him to the movies."

"What are you seeing?"

"I don't know. I'll have to ask what he wants to see."

"No, don't ask him. It's so much more romantic if you take him to a movie you know he'll like. What kind of movies do you think he likes?"

"Old. Black and white. You know, classics."

"That's kind of a challenge. But you know there is that Kafka movie."

"Kafka?"

"Yeah, you remember, they made us read him in high school." I guess she forgot that part of the reason she wrote my reports in high school was that I didn't read the books. "It's playing at the Mega-Mega Twenty-Eight. Are you having dinner first?"

"He gets off at seven, so I'm thinking maybe a late dinner afterward."

"Late dinners are so romantic."

I had everything I needed and was standing at my front door ready to leave. "I have to go to work. I'm going to hang up now."

"Call me from your car."

"Don't you have kids to take care of?"

"Arthur's making them chocolate chip pancakes so I can have some me-time."

"Maddy, your me-time should be about you, not me."

"Men. You never understand anything. I wish I had a sister."

"Sucks to be you," I said. Then I hung up.

CHAPTER TWENTY

It was incredibly sweet of Dog to ask me out to the movies. It is incredibly sad that there's no such thing as a good movie anymore. Of course, I didn't say that to him. I kept it to myself. My movie collection was entirely pre-twenty-first century. I know this is practically un-American, but I just can't relate to the problems of a superhero. I suppose I might enjoy that kind of film more if I had a superpower—like being able to kill people with the flick of a limp wrist—but so far that hasn't happened.

I'd like to see more movies about everyday people. People with problems real people might actually have. *Mildred Pierce,* for example; I'm sure lots of people have sociopathic children who steal their husbands and then murder them. *I Married a Dead Man* is another favorite. An unmarried pregnant woman is in a train crash and misidentified as a newly widowed pregnant woman, who is then taken in by her 'dead husband's' family. Now, that's what I call realism. The choice between a lifetime of lies and abject poverty—that I can connect with.

Unfortunately, Dog and I were going to see *Roach Man,* which was not based on a comic but was instead a 3-D adaptation of Kafka's *Metamorphosis.* According to the standee in the lobby it was "the story of a young man who wakes up as an enormous cockroach after ingesting an experimental pesticide. At first, everyone despises his hideous appearance. Then, after he saves his family and the world from an infestation of verminous rats, people begin to accept him." I only hoped the movie was as heartwarming as the write up.

Oddly enough, Dog seemed convinced I would love the film. I couldn't imagine what I might have said that would lead him to believe I'd like a film about a bug with superpowers. Not that it really mattered. What I was looking forward to most was sitting next to Dog in the dark. I would have been happy to stay home and fuck all night, but Dog had this idea that we should go on a proper date. I got that he was serious about me, and I was feeling pretty serious about him, too. What he wasn't quite understanding was that 'sleazy hookup' was a quality I was looking for in a boyfriend. After the way we met, I knew that Dog gave great sleazy hookup. I just wanted him to do it more often.

Of course, I was wearing my favorite theater-going outfit. A Bette Davis tee in size XXS, a vintage pair of pegged jeans and, the icing on the cake, silver glitter high-tops. I think Dog actually liked the outfit, at least a little, when he picked me up he said, "Wow."

The theater we went to was the Ming's Mega-Mega Twenty-Eight. Twenty-eight movie theaters in one location. It took five minutes to read the NOW PLAYING board that rose for a story and a half above the box office. Just inside, beyond the box office, was an enormous lobby. It had enough room for a crowd of people going to any of twenty-eight movies *and* a Chevy Camaro. The car, was being raffled off, though, I think the raffle began in 2011. Certainly the car had been sitting there for years. They might have given away other

Camaros, I wasn't sure, but this one, I knew, had been there forever.

We got in line for popcorn and sodas. "I never get popcorn. The prices are absolutely absurd. Five dollars for popcorn? Popcorn and a blow job, maybe." That made me think of Connie and I shivered.

"Don't worry, I'm paying," Dog said. "I know it's expensive, but it's, you know, part of the experience."

"Well, in that case can we have candy, too?"

"Yes, we can have candy."

I smiled at him ridiculously. We were planning a bite to eat after the movie and then home to fuck. I wondered if I couldn't convince him to skip the bite to eat. Popcorn and candy would be plenty for me.

"It's so great to be on a date with you," I said.

"It's great to be on a date with you."

Oh my Gawd! He was smiling at me in the same ridiculous way I was smiling at him. I couldn't believe it. I wasn't sure I'd ever felt exactly this way before. I mean, I'd had crushes, infatuations, an obsession or two, but this, this felt real in a way nothing had before.

"Turn around and look the other way," Dog said suddenly. He was looking across the lobby at a small group of people. "My parents. Turn around."

I turned around, facing away from the people he'd been looking at. What were we going to do? He didn't want to see his family, and after what they'd put him through the other night I couldn't blame him. I mean, it was mainly his dad, but his mom and sister sounded just a little bit off, too. I certainly was not ready to run into them.

I realized then that I'd never actually met anyone's parents. None of my boyfriends had lasted long enough for that to even be an option. And certainly, I hadn't been seeing Dog long enough to meet his parents. Thank

Gawd he decided to hide from them. Hopefully they were going to a different movie. Once they were in their theater and we were in ours everything would be—

"Dougie! You didn't say you were going to the movies tonight!" It was a woman's voice, possibly older. My stomach sank and I was bracing myself to turn around and meet his family when she asked, "Are you here alone?"

"Yeah," he said.

What the fuck? He was here alone? I couldn't stop myself. I took my heel and jammed it backward into his calf.

"Ugggh," I heard him say.

"What's wrong? Are you all right?"

"I'm fine, Mom. You know maybe that line over there would be faster."

"Oh, no, this one's fine."

"Why are you here alone on a Friday night?" Another woman, younger. Must be his sister. "Being gay has to be more fun than that. Please tell me it's more fun than that."

"See Dora, I told you it was a lonely life." A man, older.

"What are you seeing, Dougie?" his mom asked.

"*Roach Man.*"

"So are we!" his sister said.

"What a coincidence," Dog said. He sounded angry.

"Can I help you?" It took me a moment to realize that the kid behind the counter was trying to sell me popcorn. Popcorn I was no longer interested in.

Finally, I looked at him and said, "Sorry, dear, lost my wallet." And then I walked away.

###

I couldn't believe this was happening. As we walked into the movie theater loaded down with popcorn and candy and sodas, I tried to think of ways to murder my sister. Unfortunately, the police would probably suspect Arthur and, since I couldn't leave my niece and nephew completely orphaned, I'd end up confessing. Murder was out of the question. I'd just have to find a way to make her life miserable.

I maneuvered myself next to her and whispered, "What do you think you're doing?"

"Going to the movies. Where's your boyfriend?"

"He's here somewhere. I can't believe you did this."

"I did this? Why did you say you were alone?"

"I'm not ready to introduce Lionel to Dad."

"So you just walked away from him?"

"Shut up."

"Wait, was he that guy in the silver sneakers and the teeny-tiny T-shirt?"

"I said, shut up."

"Oh my God, I can't wait for Dad to get a good look—"

"What are you two whispering about?" my mom asked.

"Nothing," we said at the same time. We sounded about eleven.

Lionel had to be somewhere in the theater, but every time I looked around to find him I couldn't. I sent him a text asking where he was, but he hadn't answered it by the time I had to turn my phone off. During the previews, I realized there wasn't anything to do except keep an eye out for Lionel and hope for the best.

The movie was actually pretty good. It was the first time I'd ever rooted for vermin, which made it kind of interesting. The rats were disgusting, so it was good that Roach Man squished, pulverized, annihilated and generally destroyed them. Of course, there was a scene right at the end that let us know the rats would be back for *Roach Man 2*.

As soon as the movie ended, I'd say good-bye to my family and find Lionel. Hopefully, he didn't hate my guts too much. I mean, the fact that my dad was at the movies with me less than a week after finding out I was gay was so much more than I could've expected. And I just knew that if he met Lionel this soon, we'd be back at square one. Lionel would be too much for my dad. Way too much. He wouldn't understand. I wasn't even sure I understood half the time. And while my mother kept saying my father's heart was better than we thought, I didn't think two big shocks in one week would be good for him.

"Well, that was my idea of a movie," my dad said as we stood in the lobby. "A strong masculine man protecting his family and his community."

"You didn't notice the part where his family rejected him because he was different and then, gradually, came to accept him?" my mom said, pointedly.

"Give it a rest, Dora."

"I thought he had very well-developed abs for an insect," Maddy said. "What did you think Dougie?"

"It was good," I said. I was kinda busy looking around for Lionel. Maybe he was hiding in the men's room. "It made me want to wash my hands."

"Oh, I know," said my mom. "I've never been so thankful for anti-bacterial soap in my life."

"I'm going to the men's room. I'll see you guys later."

"We're going out for ribs. You should come with us," Maddy said.

"Oh, I, um…"

"You wash your hands, Dougie, we'll talk about it

when you come out."

There wasn't anything to do but go to the men's room, which was on the far side of the lobby. I hoped Lionel was in there so we could make a plan on how to get back to our interrupted date.

Since the movie had just gotten out, there were a couple of men in the rest room, with new ones kept coming in and out. I went to the sink and washed my hands. I didn't see Lionel anywhere. I tried to look under the two-stall doors to see if he was using one of them. I knew he was wearing a pair of plaid Vans, so it was easy to figure out if he was or wasn't in a stall. And he wasn't.

So where was he?

I dried my hands on the sides of my jeans—since all they had were those ineffective blowing machines—and got out my phone to call Lionel. He didn't answer. The call went directly to voicemail—although at first I wasn't sure, because he didn't have the normal kind of 'Hi this is Lionel please leave a message" message. No, his message was a man with a British accent saying, "I've said it before and I'll say it again. No more fucking Abba." And then there was a tone to let me know I could speak. It took me a moment.

"Um, hi, Lionel. Where are you? The movie's over and I can't find you. Call me."

I clicked off. Maybe he just hadn't turned his phone back on. Maybe he was still in the theater. I would have gone to check, but when I walked out of the men's room my family was standing about ten feet away waiting for me.

I walked over and before they could say anything I said, "Guys, I've got some things to do so I can't go out with you to eat."

My mother elbowed my father. Hard.

"Son, we want you to come to dinner with us. In

fact, we insist you come to dinner with us."

Wow. Was my dad coming around? Or at least not hating me as much. I knew I should say no—but I didn't. And so I abandoned Lionel in the middle of yet another date. Crap. Double crap.

CHAPTER TWENTY-ONE

"He did it to you *again*?" Carlos screamed when I called to ask for a ride. "He's such a bastard."

"His family was there. He freaked."

"Big deal. My family threatened to have the Mexican Mafia kill me and I didn't leave anyone in the middle of a date."

"Were you on a date when they said that?"

"No, but that doesn't matter. I would never let a death threat get in the way of getting laid." I actually believed that. "So, you're not going to forgive him again, are you?"

"No. Never."

"I think that's a good idea. There are so many other tunas in the sea."

"Fish. Fish in the sea."

"What? A tuna's not a fish?"

"You're right, Carlotta, there are a lot of tunas in the sea."

I couldn't argue with him. At that particular moment I was sad more than anything else. When it came down to it there wasn't a whole lot to my relationship with Dog. We'd had sex two times. Two and a half if you count phone sex. Had two aborted dates. And, really, that was it. There wasn't a lot to be angry about. There was also no reason to keep trying. Obviously, Dog had things to work out.

The only upside to the evening was that I didn't have to sit through *Roach Man.* Instead, I snuck into a screening of *The Incredible Shrinking Bride.* It was an odd kind of horror comedy about a hundred and twenty-pound bride (played by a ninety-eight pound actress) who wanted to lose ten pounds before her wedding in order to fit into her fantasy wedding dress. Unfortunately, the weight loss medications given to her by a friend who works at a ginormous pharmaceutical company cause her to shrink, and shrink, and shrink. Fortunately, her fiancé loves her deeply and is still willing to marry her, even though by the end of the movie she's the size of a postage stamp. It was strangely sweet with the catch phrase, "Love is never small."

It also pointed up the failings in my romance with Dog. I knew in my heart that Dog wouldn't marry me if I were the size of a postage stamp, and that meant we shouldn't be together. Of course, if I were actually the size of a postage stamp, I wouldn't let him marry me. I mean, for one thing our sex life would be incredibly disappointing.

The Incredibly Shrinking Bride must have gotten out after *Roach Man,* because when I turned my phone back on there was a message from Dog asking where I was and telling me to call. There was also a text.

STUCK HAVING DINNER WITH FAMILY. CAN WE MEET LATER?

Um, no, we can't meet later, was my first thought. *Um, no, we can't meet ever,* was my second. I texted back, LOSE MY PHONE NUMBER.

"Frida needs gas, do you have any money?" Carlos

asked. He was wearing his waiter's gear from The Bird having slipped out to get me during his dinner break.

"How do you not have money for gas? Aren't you making tips tonight?"

"It's horrible without you. I do all the work and Andrew gets all the tips."

"You should pool tips."

"I brought that up and Andrew said, 'Only communists pool tips.'" Which was stupid since I had a strong feeling there wasn't much tipping happening in communist countries.

I took a ten out of my pocket and passed it over to Carlos. "Is it safe to turn her off long enough to fill up?"

"We'll have to take that chance." We both started scanning the streets for a gas station. Carlos didn't let that stop him expressing his opinion. "You know, Lynette, he was the wrong guy for you. Mixed marriages never work."

"We're not *that* different."

"In order to make a relationship work you have to have things in common. You need a man who knows all the lyrics to *Evita*—the Madonna version, and can name at least three Bette Davis movies, and thinks Tim Gunn is the sexiest daddy in America."

"I don't want to be with someone exactly like me. Wouldn't that be boring?"

"I don't know, Lynette. The boys I see who make it as a couple, well, they're practically twins. Or father and son if there's an age difference."

"I'm not really into incest."

"Ah, you're so conservative."

"Besides, the last thing in the world I need right now is a boyfriend. I'm probably going to lose my job. Two jobs in two weeks. I need to focus on my professional life, not my love life."

Then I told him the story of Connie. Part way through we found a gas station and Carlos pumped ten bucks of gas into Frida. We got back into the car and he tried to start her up. She moaned in a really distressed way. Then he began speaking to her in Spanish. That must have helped, since the engine turned over.

"Finish your story, Lynette," he said as we pulled back onto the street.

"Well, she said she wouldn't tell anyone I was gay if I told people she gives amazing blowjobs. And then today at work, well, I didn't *say* she gave me a blow job exactly, but I sure let people think she did."

"Do you think she's like the girl in the movie?"

"What girl?"

"The one who really liked blowjobs because she had an extra hooha deep down in her throat?"

"I don't have any reason to believe that there's anything unusual about Connie's anatomy."

"So you think all women have hoohas down there?"

"No, I don't think that at all. I think she's a very unhappy alcoholic who is desperate for human affection."

"Or she just likes giving blow jobs." Carlos said, shrugging. "But you don't have anything to worry about. They can't fire you for being gay. It's illegal in California. I googled it."

"They also don't have to tell you why they're firing you. I googled that."

"You mean they can fire you for being gay as long as they don't tell you they're firing you for being gay? That's terrible. Why did we even bother to fight for our rights?"

"Carlotta, *we* didn't actually do anything. *We* don't even vote."

"I don't have time to be on no jury."

I promised myself I'd register to vote. Someday. Soon.

We were almost to The Bird when Carlos asked, "What are you going to do if he texts you again?"

"Ignore it."

"And if he calls you?"

"Won't answer."

"And if he knocks on your door?"

"Pretend not to be home."

"And if you run into him on the street?"

"Jump into the bushes and hide."

"Good boy."

Sitting in the center of the outdoor mall's vast parking lot was a restaurant called the Rib Cage. It was part of the same open-air mall as the movie theater, so my family and I just walked over from the multiplex. The outside was gray and gloomy, looking something like Alcatraz. The inside split the difference between federal prison and cannibal's dungeon.

The five of us were led to a large round table in the corner. Our waiter was dressed like a prison guard and explained the "rules" to us newbs while giving out menus with the bold heading, LAST MEAL.

We'd all been there before, so it wasn't hard to decide what we wanted. My dad and I ordered the Maximum Sentence: full slab of ribs, two pieces of chicken, fries and a tiny cup of coleslaw. Maddy had the Parole Denied: a half slab, breast of chicken, fries and a tiny cup of coleslaw. My mom ordered the Solitary Confinement: a half slab of ribs with fries and a tiny cup of coleslaw. And Arthur ordered the Community Service: a chopped chicken salad, but asked that they hold the chicken. Like he did every time we ate with Arthur, my dad muttered something to the effect that he should learn to eat like a man.

"Dad, be nice," I said under my breath.

"Dougie has been playing softball," my sister said.

"Why would you keep that a secret?" my dad asked.

"Oh, um, it's a gay league."

"A what? Why would—" I think my mother kicked him under the table, since he ended his sentence with an "Ugh."

"I was on a team, but now I'm playing as a free agent."

"What happened? Why did you leave your team?" My dad again. He couldn't resist talking sports, which was why Maddy brought it up. Throwing me a bone, I guess. "Were they that bad?"

"Crappy captain."

"Why didn't they ask you to be captain?"

"They might."

"If they've got any sense at all, they will."

"Thanks, Dad."

Suddenly, my dad went "Ugh" again. He glared at my mother. Then asked, "Are you...um, seeing anyone, Dougie?" The frown on his face was epic.

"Not right now."

"I didn't want to ask that. Your mother made me."

"You want your son to be happy, don't you?" my mother asked.

"I think he might be happier if we didn't ask those questions."

"You guys don't need to ask me any questions, it's really okay."

My dad seemed to breathe a sigh of relief, one that Maddy immediately strangled. "Dougie was on a date tonight, but he just dumped the guy the minute he saw us."

"What? That's terrible," my mom said.

I glared at Maddy. My impulse was to call her a ratfink just like I had when I was eight and she'd tell on me. Which she did a lot. It felt foolish, but I almost did it. Then I realized they were all giving me very disappointed looks. Even my dad.

"Are you ashamed of us, son?" he asked.

"No, I—it was only a second date. And I didn't feel ready." Then I very pointedly added, "Despite what some people think."

"Are you ashamed of your date?" my mother asked.

"No," I said. God, that was weak. "He's just different, that's all."

"And you didn't think we'd approve."

"He didn't think Dad would approve."

There was a short pause and then my dad went "Ugh" again. "Oh for God's sake, Dora. I'm going to have a bruise the size of Catalina." Then he stood up. "Come with me, son. We're going for a walk."

"Oh Dad, we don't need to do that."

"If we don't, your mother will break my ankle. Come on."

I followed him out of the restaurant. Outside, we stood awkwardly in the parking lot between a Mini Cooper and a Hyundai SUV. I waited for him to say something. It took a little bit for him to warm up.

"Your mother, she reminded me of something...I don't know that I've ever told you this, but back in the nineteen-forties your grandmother wanted to marry a Catholic boy and he wanted to marry her. His family wouldn't let them get married. My grandparents weren't too happy about it either. So your grandmother married someone else and they were never what you'd call happy.

She never really got over the Catholic boy. It seems like a very foolish thing today. The idea that two young people would let their families interfere with their happiness over religion, and, worse, two religions that are more alike than they are different."

He cleared his throat and continued, "I always felt bad for my parents."

"It's a sad story."

"Then you understand what I'm saying. Good, we'll go back inside now."

"Wait, Dad, what is it you're saying? Exactly."

"It doesn't matter what I think about...the way you are. It doesn't matter if I'm *ever* comfortable with who you are. Or with who you...um, love. What matters is that you're happy."

"Thank you, Dad."

"When you first think about having kids you think about all the ways they'll make you happy. But then you have them and you realize it's much more important to make them happy. That it's your job to help them learn how to be happy. I may have forgotten that...for a while."

"It's all right, Dad."

He shrugged like none of this mattered. We stood there feeling awkward. I wanted to hug him, but I knew that wasn't what men—*Wait,* I thought, *I don't have to follow those rules anymore.* I grabbed my dad and hugged him tight. He put up with it for a few seconds then wiggled away.

"Judas Priest, I'm hungry. How about you?"

CHAPTER TWENTY-TWO

That Saturday, I'd only had the bar open for about an hour when Pepper showed up grimacing like a witch who'd lost her magic beans. Storming over to the bar, she said, "We have to talk." She came behind the bar and then went into the little storage room. I glanced at the four regulars I had sitting there and said, "Be right back."

I slumped into the storage room, ready to lose my job. Apparently, simply not denying she'd given me a blow job wasn't enough for Connie, she must have started telling people I was gay. Beginning with Pepper. This week wasn't going especially well. No Dog, no job. Life was really sucking.

"So, Connie has been talking…" Pepper said.

"I'd hoped she wasn't going to."

"Connie? She's got the biggest mouth in Southern California."

"So, I'm fired?"

"Only if it's true."

I could continue the lie, but really, what was the point. My little experiment in being closeted had failed. "Yes, it's true. I'm gay."

The look Pepper gave me was withering. "Of course

you're gay. But why in the world would you let Connie give you a blow job?"

"What? No. No. She didn't. She offered, but I said no. Actually, I think I said, 'Get off me, bitch.'"

Pepper's face unfroze. "Well, that's a relief."

"So I'm not fired? It's okay that I'm gay?"

"You thought I was going to fire you for being gay?" Pepper burst out laughing. "I hired you *because* you're gay."

"You did? Wait, you never thought I was—"

"I saw you at The Bird one time. I mean, the butch act was cute, but mainly what I need is a day bartender who's not going to try to sleep with every piece of tail that comes in here. I want to attract more women, and creepy bartenders hitting on them all day long isn't going to help."

I wondered for a moment if she and Bob Grottoli had had some kind of business conference and decided gay guys working in straight bars and straight guys working in gay bars was the way to go. It was one of those ideas that made sense and didn't make sense at the same time.

"So that's why you didn't call my reference?"

"Your fake reference you mean? I knew exactly what you were doing, so I didn't waste my time. I did call Bob Grottoli, though."

"And he gave me a good reference?"

"No, he said you were a mouthy asshole. I thought that was a quality that might come in handy at V-Bar."

"So...should I pretend to be straight for the customers?"

"Do what you're comfortable with."

"Really?"

"Yeah, really. I don't give a shit. Just no blow jobs in the storage room from Connie. Actually, no blow jobs in the storage room from anyone, okay? I don't want to run that kind of place."

I went back out to the bar and glanced at everyone's drink to see who needed a refill. Bobby G. needed a fresh drink so I went ahead and made him a Smirnov and Coke. I set it in front of him saying, "By the way, I'm gay."

"Does that affect my drink in some way?" That's the thing about alcoholics, they have their priorities straight.

"Of course not. Although, I have no idea how you drink those. Did you have your stomach replaced with a tin can?"

"Ha!" Bobby G. laughed.

"Also, that one's on me."

That caught the attention of the others at the bar. Tran guzzled the rest of his wine and then pushed his glass toward me. I poured him another house wine on the rocks.

"What are we celebrating?"

"I'm gay."

Tran looked across the bar and called out, "Hey, Walt, Leo here is gay. So no fag jokes."

Walt, a regular I'd only met that morning, shrugged and kept watching ESPN. He didn't look the sort who told jokes of any sort

The regulars didn't seem too surprised to find out I was gay. Carlos was wrong, I wasn't the Meryl Streep of closet cases. It used to bother me that everyone knew I was gay before I came out to them. But now I wondered if it didn't actually make life easier.

My phone vibrated in my pocket. I pulled it out and glanced down at it. Another text from Dog. I knew I should probably just block his number. In fact, I promised myself I'd do it. Tomorrow. Or Monday. Or maybe he'd just figure out I wasn't going to respond and start leaving me alone.

I flipped through the texts he'd sent. He did seem sorry. I could imagine Carlos scolding me. Dog was embarrassed by me, that was so, so obvious. Dating someone who was basically embarrassed by me was not a good idea in any universe. Seriously, try to have self-esteem in the face of that. When I looked up from my phone, I saw that Connie had walked in. I began building her usual drink.

"So are we going to have as much fun as yesterday?" she asked, with a wink.

"You told Pepper you gave me a blow job, didn't you?"

"I couldn't help it. She came into the restaurant after the bar closed with three different guys trying to get into her pants. I mean, she could leave one or two for the rest of us."

"Hey Connie, you hear the news?" Bobby G. asked. "Leo is a queer."

"What? No. Why would you tell people something like that?"

I was kind of stumped. Could she possibly think it was wrong to tell people I was gay, but absolutely right to discuss her imaginary oral sex skills? Was that the upside-down world she lived in? I set her drink in front of her and said, "That'll be three fifty." She gave me a rather frigid look and paid. Three drinks later though, she started getting friendly again.

"Aw right, you know how they always say that gay guys give the best blow jobs? I want you to prove it. We need to have a suck-off."

"Darling, I don't think so."

"We need a bisexual, though. You suck him off and he'll say whether that was good, and then I'll suck him off and he'll say whether that was good. And whichever one is good-er, I mean better, is the winner."

"And what do we win Connie?"

She chewed on that for a moment. "Well if the guy's cute enough, we've already won." That she found hysterical and guffawed loudly. "So where do we find a bisexual? Is there an app for that?"

###

Lionel wouldn't answer my texts or my phone calls. I thought about going over to his apartment, but was afraid he'd just tell me to go away. Well, not afraid. I knew he'd tell me to go away. And I couldn't blame him. I'd blown it. I wished there was a way I could fix it all, but I had no idea how.

After dinner with my family, I barely got any sleep. Staring at the ceiling, I kept thinking about what Maddy had said, that I was ashamed of Lionel. I said I wasn't but...wow, maybe I was. I didn't want to be. I didn't feel anything like that when we were alone. But then I knew what other people would think. I knew what my dad would think. I knew what guys on the team would think. And I guess, that's what I would have thought, too. Before Lionel.

But, why? I mean, what difference did it make? What was the deal with not liking femme guys? Yeah, for a lot of straight people it wasn't surprising. Lionel was clearly gay, and if you had a problem with gay guys, you had a big problem with Lionel. But, what about gay guys? Why did we—

And then I had a weird thought. Femme guys scared us. They scared us because we were afraid of being like them. We were afraid of being obvious. And that was part of the whole being in the closet bull. Not liking femme guys was really about not liking ourselves. Wow.

The next morning, I dragged myself to work. I felt better after thinking things through. But, man, I was tired. While I dragged myself though the day, I got a couple of messages from Tim and Fetch. Both messages said that the team wanted to buy me a drink at The Bird after I got off work. I hoped that meant they'd buy me *one* drink. There were ten guys on the team. I didn't want ten drinks. It was about six more than I really enjoyed.

Sure enough, when I got to The Bird, Fetch and Tim had a draft and two shots of tequila waiting for me. After our talk with Bob, I was pretty sure I was there to say goodbye to the team and maybe hash things over for a last time, but the first thing I said when I saw Tim and Fetch was, "I blew it with Lionel."

"It's probably not a bad thing," Tim said.

"It was never going to last. Better that it ends now," Fetch agreed.

"I don't think that's right. I think it is a bad thing. A bad thing I wish I could fix." I was tempted to talk to them about the things I was thinking the night before, but that temptation faded by the time I finished my first beer. Very soon the entire team was there. I tried turning down additional shots, but it was a challenge. Larry Lamour was doing his act, so we couldn't talk a lot. The team genuinely seemed sad that I wouldn't be playing with them anymore.

I was blitzed when I heard Larry Lamour say my name. I spun around to look at him. I gave him a strong "Huh?" look, which made him repeat, "I'm going on my break now so I'm going to hand the microphone over to you, Dog."

"Me?"

Fetch and Tim gave me a shove and I was on my way to the piano. Larry handed me the mike. I turned around and looked at the team and the other people in the bar. I didn't know what was going on. What did they want me to do?

"I don't sing so I hope that's not what you're expecting."

The team laughed like that was a great joke. Then a couple of them started to yell, "Speech, speech." The regulars who weren't on the team started to clap, though some of them just looked confused. Almost as confused as I was.

"Well, I guess I should say that it's meant a lot to me playing with you guys..." That brought a round of laughter. "...playing *softball* with you guys, I mean. I'm going to be a free agent, so I'll still be seeing you all. We just won't be on the same team."

"No!" Fetch yelled. Then Tim followed with another "No!" And then some of the other guys on the team started. "No!" "NO!"

"Okay, okay...that's really nice, guys, but there's no way I can stay on the team. I think you all know why."

"Get rid of Chuckie!"

"We already talked to Bob about that and it's not going to happen."

That brought a round of boos. And an idea into my head.

"Look, if you want to get rid of Chuckie, it will have to be his idea. Anyone know how to make that happen?"

The room went quiet. *What would have to happen in order to get Chuckie to quit?* I wondered. Nothing came immediately to mind. Chuckie was stubborn, the kind of person who didn't let go. It was impossible to imagine him quitting. I wondered what he'd think of the team trying to figure out a way to get rid of him.

And then an idea began to come together. Chuckie hated the idea of not being liked. The whole way he'd handled the conflict with Lionel, he needed everyone to back him up, right or wrong. So maybe all we had to do was let him know we didn't want him. Maybe if he knew—

"Hey guys, I might have an idea."

CHAPTER TWENTY-THREE

"Lynette, you need to come to The Bird," Carlos said, when I clicked on, barely giving me time to say hello.

"Darling, I can't. I'm banned."

"Lance isn't going to pay any attention to that. You have to come. He's going to give you a free drink."

"Ah well, free alcohol...um, no. It's Sunday, the Birdmen are going to be there. I'll come another night." The Birdmen and Dog. And I didn't want to see Dog. That was a chapter of my life that was closed. A very short chapter.

"There's a rumor going around they're going to kick Chuckie off the team."

"Did you start that rumor?" Most of the rumors Carlos talked about were actually ones he started.

"No, but I'm spreading it. Come on Lynette, don't you want to see Chuckie kicked off the team?"

Did I want to see that? Did I care? No, I didn't. Not really. Not if it meant having to see Dog. The last place in the world I was going to go that afternoon was The Bird. If I really wanted to witness revenge, I'd just re-watch *Mean Girls*. In fact, that was a great plan for a Sunday afternoon. Ice cream and *Mean Girls*.

"Carlotta, I don't need to see them kick Chuckie off the team. You can tell me about it later in excruciating detail."

"Maybe it's not you who needs to see Chuckie, maybe it's Chuckie who needs to see you."

"What do you mean?"

"Think about it, Lynette. Chuckie is getting kicked off the team. Won't it be so much worse if he sees that you're there, watching."

That was actually a good point. Chuckie would hate that I was there. Dog might not hate that I was there, though. Of course, with a little effort, I could make him hate that I was there. Maybe a little real-life revenge would be more satisfying than *Mean Girls* revenge.

"Okay, if I'm coming over there, I have to figure out what to wear."

"Hurry up, darling! You don't want to miss the show."

He can say hurry up all he wants. When it comes getting dressed, I will not be rushed. I went into the bathroom and took a quick shower, shaved, brushed my teeth and perfumed myself. Then I went back into my bedroom and threw the closet doors open. Oddly, Larry Lamour's talking about how you had to figure out how to be yourself and not just the person you thought other people wanted you to be popped into my silly little head. Who was I being? Me? Or the me I thought I should be? Or was the real me someone who picked up personas and dropped them at will?

Of course, this is exactly the wrong sort of thing to think about when choosing an outfit. Especially when I already had other things I had to consider. I needed to wear something that said, "Fuck you, you're getting what you deserve," to Chuckie, and "Aren't you sorry you screwed up," to Dog, while at the same time managing to express the true, authentic me.

Skinny jeans came to mind right away. I had them in three shades of blue, burgundy, white, slate, black and lavender. Okay, that decision might require some thought. I looked down at my shoes. Aside from the red pumps—the heel of which was now wobbly—I had four other pairs of high heels. Black, bone, navy, and white sandals with a plastic daisy covering the toes. Unfortunately, even though my ankle was much improved, there was no way I was wearing a heel. Though the daisy sandal with the lavender skinny jeans would have made a bold statement.

But then, maybe a bold statement wasn't called for. Maybe I'd just wear the black skinny jeans with my teal cashmere sweater (I'd had such excellent taste during the all too brief period when I'd had credit cards) along with my pink Chuck Taylors. That was pretty toned down. Or at least my idea of toned down. I got dressed and then spent another half an hour in the bathroom getting my hair to swoop in exactly the way I liked.

It was just about the time the Birdmen usually showed up at The Bird when I left my apartment. I wasn't sure whether this was a good idea or a bad one, but it was now an idea that was going to happen. If it didn't go well, I'd blame Carlos for everything. In fact, that should be my new motto: Blame others.

When I walked into The Bird, Chuckie was already at the bar. The dining room was empty and the bar area only had a few customers. Chuckie turned and saw me as I walked in. I ignored his stare and marched past him, choosing a stool at the far end of the bar. Lance started toward me. Chuckie tried to stop him, "Uh, Lance—"

"I'll be with you in a minute, Chuckie. I've got a customer." Chuckie's face grew sour. Well, sour-er.

"What can I get you, Lionel?" Lance asked me.

"Sapphire Martini, straight up, four olives, whis—"

"I know, sweetheart, I haven't forgotten." He gave me a nice smile. I wondered if the fact that I'd never had sex with him was a big mistake. On the one hand, I hated being part of a crowd. On the other, I hated missing out. Since there was obviously no Dog on my horizon, perhaps fucking Lance was a good idea. It would certainly be an interesting way to end the evening. And if I had enough martinis, I could blame them.

Down at the other end of the bar, Lance was making my drink. Chuckie had moved down a couple of stools to sit in front of the service bar. He whispered intently to Lance, who smiled at him but kept making the drink.

"Lynette, there you are," Carlos said as he approached me from behind. "I'm so happy you came."

"Chuckie's telling Lance not to serve me and Lance is ignoring him."

"You know Lance. He always beats his own drummer."

"That's 'walks to the beat of…'—never mind. So I'm not banned? Did Bob change his mind?"

Carlos shook his head. "We made up Bob's mind for him."

"How did you do that?"

"We didn't tell him."

That made me feel a bit weird. All Chuckie had to do was call Bob and I'd be thrown out. Worse, Lance and Carlos would be in trouble. Lance slid my drink in front of me. I reached into my pocket to get a twenty but he said, "That's on the house."

"No, that's fine I can pay—"

"Professional courtesy. I hear you're working at V-Bar. What is *that* like?"

Figuring he could relate to the unwanted advances of

customers, I began to tell him the story of Connie and the non-existent blow job. The story was getting some good chuckles from him, and I wasn't even embellishing—much—when suddenly I lost his attention. He was gaping at the front door.

I turned to see that the Birdmen had started walking into the bar. Fetch and Tim were in the front. The bar was quiet enough that I could hear the clacking of their shoes against the floor. Their shoes. My first thought was that they must be wearing cleats. *Did softball players even wear cleats?* I wondered. I had no idea. Then I looked down.

Oh my Gawd! My jaw dropped. I was lucky I didn't bruise it on the bar. They were wearing red high heels. *All* five of them. Six. Eight. Nine. Nine softball players had just walked into the bar wearing red heels. It didn't make any sense—except it did.

The Birdmen had chosen quite the variety: open-toed, sling-backs, sandals, ankle straps, wedge heels, strappy...all with coarse, un-manicured toes and hairy ankles sticking out of them. It was truly a lovely sight.

Dog brought up the rear. He'd chosen red patent leather sandals with ankle straps and platforms. He, or someone, had bedazzled them with some kind of glitter, as though he wanted to bring extra attention to himself. Even from across the bar, I could see that he'd bought the shoes too tight. His toes were flushed red, and spilled over the edges of the shoe. It looked incredibly painful and, foolishly, that made my heart bounce.

The hair on the back of my neck stood up and my eyes watered. Dog. Dog was behind this. He had to be. That was the real reason Carlos had called me to come over. Dog. My eyes grew damp and I stared at him, biting my lip. At that particular moment, I couldn't imagine anything a man could do for another man that would mean more than wearing a very painful pair of sparkly high heels.

Crap. The shoes were murder. But they seemed to be sending the message I wanted to send. I mean, messages. Two messages. Lionel sat at the far end of the bar with a martini in front of him. His face seemed guarded the moment he saw me, but when he looked down and saw the shoes it softened. His eyes met mine and we just looked at each other. Really looked. It was the best feeling I'd had in a long while. And totally worth the pain shooting up my legs.

I pulled my eyes away from him and looked over at Chuckie. He was pale and looked like he might puke. He was doing some mental arithmetic. Every single one of the Birdmen was there. All wearing red high heels. He had to know that meant we weren't going to let him bully us anymore. Slowly, he got off his stool and walked over.

"I guess this is your idea of a practical joke." He was looking at me when he said it. Then he took in the other guys. "You all look ridiculous, by the way."

That earned him a couple of smirks but mainly silence.

"Okay, joke's over. Ha-ha. You can take those hideous things off."

The bar got quiet—or quiet for a bar. Chuckie tried staring us down. Ten of us. Finally, I said, "Chuckie, we don't want you to be team captain anymore. In fact, we don't want you on the team."

"But...I've done everything for the team. I mean, there wouldn't even be a team if it weren't for me." For a moment, he looked genuinely hurt and I worried that the team might cave if he managed to make them feel sorry for him. Heck, maybe I was going to cave. But it was only a moment. Chuckie went on the offensive, "So this is how you repay me? By kicking me off the team? By mocking me? What a bunch of losers. That's all you are, that's all you'll ever be."

Then he threw a drink in my face and walked out of The Bird. The team immediately cheered. They were patting me on the back, nearly knocking me off my shoes. I pointed myself in Lionel's direction and hobbled over.

When I got close to Lionel, I said the only logical thing I could think of to say, "Hi."

"Hi. You need a napkin." He scrambled to get a few cocktail napkins off a nearby pile. Handing them to me, he said, "Um, that's quite the statement you just made."

I shrugged. "It needed to happen."

"Well don't get all shy now, I think you deserve a few choruses of 'Ding-Dong! the Witch Is Dead'."

"Okay, that's something I've heard of." My sister and I watched *The Wizard of Oz* a lot when we were kids.

"You should be proud of yourself. I can't imagine organizing a softball team into high heels was all that simple."

"It wasn't."

Lionel looked down at my poor feet. "Don't take this the wrong way, but those shoes aren't really you."

"Nope. Not even close."

"It's a sweet gesture."

"It's a painful gesture. My father would hate it if he saw me in these shoes."

"Does that matter so much?"

"Not as much as it used to," I said, without thinking. But that was the right answer. It still mattered what my family thought. It always would. But what mattered more was what I thought. And I thought wearing high heels on this particular Sunday evening was the right thing to do.

"You can take them off now," Lionel said. "You don't need to scare anyone else with them."

I wasn't going to argue with that so I bent over and undid the buckle on each shoe, then stepped out of them. It was such a relief. I could feel my feet stretching out again where they'd been strapped in. They felt like caged animals escaping from a zoo.

"Can we get out of here?" I suggested.

"Shouldn't you spend some time with your team?"

"I don't think they'll mind too much if I slip out."

But just then, Lance came down with a new drink for Lionel and a beer and shot for me. They were on Fetch and Tim. So, that settled that. We were staying for another drink.

Larry Lamour arrived a bit later and, since enough of the guys were still wearing their heels, started out his set with that old Bowie song about putting on red shoes and dancing. He had a lot of fun improving the original lyrics.

Different members of the Birdmen kept coming by and bringing drinks for Lionel and me. Well, sometimes just me. Shots. Lots of shots. Pretty soon, I'd lost count of how many. But I didn't feel that drunk. Yeah, I was kinda hanging all over Lionel, whispering into his ear the things I wanted us to do to each other as soon as we could figure out how to leave.

That must have gotten to Lionel, because when the last round of drinks arrived he refused them, saying, "No, no, no, we have had enough. More than enough. Way too much." Which was funny, because I still didn't feel that drunk, you know? I could stand up almost straight and my words were too slurry, wait, I mean *weren't* too slurry. Yeah, that's right.

Then Lionel was leading me out of the bar. On the way out, I was sure I saw Fetch and Tim in the corner making out. About time, if you ask me. *If* I saw it. Maybe I didn't see it.

Outdoors on the sidewalk, the night was cool and totally refreshing. I couldn't believe how not-drunk I felt. It was like I'd barely had anything to drink at all. If there's one thing I can say about myself, it's that I can hold my liquor.

"Hey," I said to Lionel. "This is just like the night we met. Except we're sober-er. More sober. Not as drunk."

CHAPTER TWENTY-FOUR

We were drunk as shit.

Dog had the messed up idea that we weren't very drunk. Which was extremely messed up since he was actually way drunker than I was. I was drunk but he was, well, blotto, wasted, smashed, and very, very sloppy. I had a sort of flashback to the night we hooked up, which gave me the distinct feeling this was something he did every time he got really, really drunk. Decide he wasn't drunk. Which was kind of funny. And cute. And completely delusional.

I looked down and noticed he was still barefoot. "Where are your shoes?"

"Oh gosh, I left my pumps in the bar."

"Sandals."

"Wha?"

"You wore sandals, not pumps. They're different."

"Do they both hurt like hell?"

"They can."

"Then they're not that different."

That made him laugh. And laugh. Oh my Gawd! He was drunk! The joke wasn't that funny, after all. I decided not to worry about his sandals; Lance knew who they belonged to. He'd hang on to them. "Where are your boy shoes?"

"In my truck."

"Where's you truck?"

"That way." He pointed in three different directions, almost hitting me in the face. "About two blocks."

Since he wasn't too clear on where the truck actually was, it didn't make any sense to walk him around barefoot looking for it. I decided I'd come out and get his shoes in the morning. I pointed him toward my apartment and hoped for the best.

"I'm really, really glad I met you," he said. He was a sweet drunk. Always preferable to the "I'm going to knock your head off" kind of drunk many people turn out to be.

"I'm really, really glad I met you, too."

"Are you? Really?"

"Really."

And then we were making out on the street. A big, sloppy, drunk make-out session on the street about a half block from my apartment. There was nothing tentative about the way he was kissing me, as there had been before. He was bold, demanding and cocksure. He also kept grabbing my cock.

I pulled away. "Okay, let's not get arrested."

"I just copped a little feel."

"Yes, sweetheart, you did," I said, pulling him toward my apartment.

When we got to my front door, I opened it and eased him inside. Settling him on my sofa, I stood back and suggested, "Maybe we should have some coffee or tea."

"Why do we need to do that?"

He reached for me and I took a step back. "Because we're kind of drunk, and I'd like to remember this."

"Oh, I think we'll remember this just fine."

"That's what you said the first time."

"And I remember that. Very well. Let's do that again. Exactly that."

"Coffee or tea?"

"Coffee."

"It's instant."

"Oh. Tea."

"Tea it is."

I went into the kitchen to put the kettle on the stove, and got out a mug and a tea bag. When I turned to go back into the living room, I found Dog there, licking his lips. He grabbed me and pulled me in close. Smashing his lips to mine, his tongue slipped into my mouth, exploring, teasing. I slid my fingers into his hair and kissed him back good and hard. We kissed until the teakettle whistled behind me. I pushed away. "You're going to be a good boy and drink your tea."

"Aww, you're taking care of me. That's what a man does. A man takes care of the people he love—likes."

I raised an eyebrow at him. "I think you're pretty clear on the fact that I'm a man."

He caught my meaning and let out a dirty giggle.

"Yeah, I remember."

Then he was grabbing me again, and I hadn't had time to do much more than turn the burner off. The water was still in the kettle and the mug empty. And then Dog was on his knees, unzipping my skinny jeans, running his fingers across my belly, just under the edge of my sweater. My dick flopped out and—

Oh my Gawd!

Wrapping his big hands around my hips, he pinned me up against my kitchen wall. He had me in his mouth all the way down to the base. I put my hands around the back of his head trying to slow him down a bit, but he was strong and had every intention of doing exactly what he wanted. And what he wanted was to bring me close to orgasm and leave me hanging.

Oh my Gawd.

I was moaning, begging, telling him to keep going, and then he stopped. Looking up at me from the floor he said, "I want you to fuck me."

I smiled and said, "I remember what you like."

How could I forget?

When I woke up in the morning my mouth was dry, my head throbbing, my ass sore and well-used. Lionel and I were wrapped up in each other like pretzels. I thought about untangling myself and getting a glass of water and some aspirin, but that seemed too complicated. I lay there remembering what I could of the night before. That made me blush.

I'd been very aggressive. Pulling Lionel on top of me and insisting that he fuck me. I cringed when I thought about the things I said. But, come to think of it, there weren't a lot of ways to ask to be fucked that were subtle. No matter how you said it, it came out sounding like something out of a porno. Which had been okay three weeks before when we were just hooking up, but now I wished there was a way to say that, which didn't sound like a porno but also didn't sound like a marriage proposal. Anyway, he got the point.

I curled into him remembering how good his dick had felt inside me. We started with me on my back and I loved that, loved looking into his eyes while he fucked me, watching the pleasure from each stroke on his face. And then, after a bit, I wanted to turn over. His dick had a small kink in it and curled away from his body just slightly, just enough that I knew if he had me from behind, it would hit in just the right way. I eased him off me and rolled over onto all fours.

"You lied to me, didn't you?" he said. "They don't call you Dog because of your name, this is why they call you Dog."

I was going to answer, to disagree, but I didn't have time since he put his dick back into me. I closed my eyes, let my face fall onto the pillow and just felt, just felt as he pumped and shockwaves floated through me. Just felt him filling me up, over and over. Just felt. And then, legs shaking, toes curling, I came. I must have jizzed everywhere. I also must have made a huge noise because Lionel shushed me.

"Sweetheart, I have neighbors," he said, easing out of me and then laying down next to me.

"Oh, sorry. Did you get off?"

"Ages ago."

"Wow," I said. My dick was pretty sensitive. When I was done, I was done. Well, for at least twenty minutes. "I'm impressed," I said.

"The condom helps," Lionel said, modestly.

"I made a wet spot. I made of lot of wet spots."

"I guess you'll have to sleep over here then."

I wrapped myself around him and stayed like that all night. Until thirst finally forced me out of his bed. I padded into his kitchen, searched through the cupboards for a glass, found an empty peanut butter jar instead, and filled it with water. Running the faucet was maybe not such a good idea. Instantly, I realized I had to pee like crazy.

Hurrying back through Lionel's bedroom I popped into the bathroom and started to pee. I was halfway through when I heard Lionel giggling behind me. "Oh my Gawd, what are you doing?"

"Peeing."

"And drinking a glass of water at the same time? What goes in must come out? Is that the theory?"

"I'm thirsty."

Finally, I was done peeing, so the next most important thing was dealing with the throbbing in my head. "Do you have aspirin?"

"In the medicine cabinet."

I opened it and found the aspirin, shook out two into my hand, and then washed them down with the last of my water. I turned back and watched Lionel standing naked in the doorway.

"This is nice," I said.

"Taking aspirin?"

"No. Us, naked."

He smiled. "You're gong to have to get dressed soon though. You have to work today, don't you?"

"Yeah, I do."

"And we have to find your truck. You're going to need to wear clothes for that."

"Darn."

"What are we doing tonight?"

"What we did last night. Minus the alcohol."

"We're not going to fuck all night."

"Spoil sport. We can have dinner. Watch a movie."

"You fall asleep when I put movies in."

"I need my rest." I shrugged. "We can do anything you want."

I closed the short gap between us and pulled him into my arms. Enjoying the feel of his naked skin against mine, I kissed him. He grabbed me by my growing cock.

"How much time do you have? I wouldn't want you to start something you can't finish."

"Oh, we'll finish."

CHAPTER TWENTY-FIVE

Oh my fucking Gawd! That was my first thought in the morning. Seriously, it was. I rolled over in bed, looked straight into Dog's face, and thought, *Oh my fucking Gawd! I get to wake up to this! All the time!* Well, not all the time. It had only been a month, I shouldn't be thinking like that. But he'd been in my bed almost every night for the last two weeks. Was it too fast? We were going too fast.

But then, everything about dating Dog had been too something. Mostly that we were too different. I didn't think that anymore, though. I mean we were definitely different, but underneath it all we were kind of the same. Dog tries hard to be a good guy, and I, for some reason I don't quite grasp, try to be a good guy, too. And that, I think, is a lot more than most people have in common.

That Sunday I was going to attend my first softball game ever. And, I was going to officially meet Dog's family. This required almost an entire day of preparation. I'd already decided what to wear. I would be wearing my pink shorts with my new black and pink flamingo T-shirt and my pink Chuck Taylors. It was an outfit that was very me, but not too much me, since I wouldn't be wearing high heels, a boa and/or a tiara.

No, the big thing that was going to take up time was a craft project I'd found on YouTube...pom-poms. I'd spent all of seven minutes and thirty-four seconds learning how to make pom-poms from garbage bags, and I was all set to make them myself. At the Dollar Store I'd bought a box of white ones, a box of black ones and box of dark green ones. A pair of scissors and a box of rubber bands, and I was ready to make the props necessary for an afternoon of rah-rah-sis-boom-bah.

"There are no cheerleaders in softball," Dog said when he caught wind of what my project was about.

"Is there a rule against cheerleaders?"

"I don't think so."

"So there *can* be cheerleaders in softball."

"I guess."

"Good. Today there will be cheerleaders." And then I began cutting up trash bags with vigor. My living room quickly turned into a disaster with tiny bits of plastic everywhere, but I'd finished my first set of pom-poms. I was very pleased with myself when Dog came back from a run.

He was sweating and red in the face. "Are you sure that was a good idea? You have a game later, you don't want to use up all your energy."

"It's a warm up."

I didn't really know what he meant by that. As I understood it, the gay softball league was the sort of league where you only needed to show up with a six-pack of beer and a clean uniform. And the clean uniform was optional.

"I'm going to take a shower, then we should probably get ready to go."

"No! I only have two pom-poms. You need to take a

really long shower," I insisted. Then I got down to making eight more pom-poms in an hour. After that, I managed to miraculously get ready in a mere fifteen minutes.

It was good thing, too, since Dog was standing at the front door looking kind of growly. "I'm sorry," I said as soon as I caught a glimpse of his face. "I know we're running late. You may need to start lying to me about time. But don't let me know that you're doing it because then I'll just adjust."

"I don't think we should lie to each other."

"Oh darling, every good relationship is built on a foundation of lies. We just have to agree on which lies we tell each other. I would like you to lie to me about time. What should I lie to you about?"

"Come on, we need to get going," he said, ignoring my question. I grabbed my bag of pom-poms and we were out the door.

It wasn't until we were in the truck and on our way to Tustin that he said, "You weren't really serious, were you? About lying to each other?"

Honestly, I wasn't all that sure if I was serious. Maybe I was; maybe I wasn't. It did seem that a certain amount of lying, or lying within bounds, might be good for a relationship. Absolute honesty could be a disastrous problem, after all.

"I'm not sure if I was serious," I said, honestly.

"Oh." Dog thought for a moment and then said, "I think we should always be honest with each other."

"Do you like my outfit?" I asked.

"What? Wait, don't change the subject."

"I'm not changing the subject. Do you like my outfit?"

"Yeah, it's fine."

"No, it's not. I'm wearing pink shorts and pink sneakers to meet your family."

"It's not important, Lionel."

"Exactly. That's why you said my outfit is fine when you really think it's not. That's why you told a lie."

"Oh," he said. I watched as he thought it through. The very real consequences of telling people the truth all the time. "This is hard."

"It is," I agreed. I thought again about the things that Larry Lamour said about being yourself. It was hard to be yourself. It was hard for me and it was hard for Dog. And it was going to be hard for us to be ourselves, together.

"It's all hard, Doug."

He slipped his hand over mine on the seat. "It is. But it's going to be worth it."

"It is already."

We arrived at the field. It had actually rained just days before, so we could see the mountains in the distance. I don't know which range. We don't see it often, so it seems kind of pointless to learn its name. The mountains are pretty, though, all jagged and blue in the distance.

I was as nervous as a two-dollar hooker in church. I didn't know what to expect. I mean, Dog's family sounded nice. And he said things were getting a lot better than they'd been. But my whole experience of family was my mom dying and my dad not really giving a shit about me, so, even if they were really nice, I wasn't sure how to act around that. I mean, yes, I should be nice back. But what one person thought was nice wasn't necessarily what another person thought was nice.

Dog and I walked across the parking lot toward a minivan disgorging a bunch of people. I'd barely gotten to look at Dog's family when we were at the movie theater, so it was kind of the first time I'd ever really looked at them. His mom and dad were in their late fifties to early sixties, I wasn't sure which. They both had a fair amount of gray hair and slightly spreading middles. His sister, Maddy, looked a lot like Dog. She had his same coloring, dark hair and brown eyes, and his same broad shoulders, which she probably hated but kind of worked. Her husband, Arthur, trailed behind carrying a small cooler.

As they got closer, I could see that Dog's mom had a really sweet look on her face, Maddy appeared to be amused by the whole thing, while his dad looked determined and, perhaps, a little bit angry. Suddenly, I felt like the whole pom-pom idea was incredibly stupid. I wanted to run back to the car and shove the bag I was carrying into the trunk, and pretend I'd never brought them.

But then it was too late. Dog's dad was barreling down at me in the most uncomfortable way. I wondered what he was going to do when he got to me. *Hit me? Yell at me? Oh Gawd, this was going to be a disaster.*

###

Before we left the house, I called Maddy and told her that Lionel was coming to the game. And then I asked her to do something that I wouldn't normally do. "Could you gossip about me?"

"I don't gossip."

"Seriously, you don't gossip? Look, just make sure that Mom and Dad know about Lionel and that they have some idea what Lionel is like."

"Okay…" she said, doubtfully.

"What?"

"Don't expect it to go too well. I mean, Mom will be

okay, but Dad's really been through a lot this… has it only been a month? Oh my God."

"I'm dating Lionel, though. I can't hide him."

"Can't keep hiding him, you mean."

"Shut up."

"Don't worry. It'll be fine. Or it won't."

"Thanks."

And then I was walking across the parking lot with Lionel. Lionel and his pink shorts and his bag of pom-poms. I just knew my dad was going to hate him, and that was going to suck. Worse than that, I was leaving Lionel alone with my dad for the entire game. Crap. Why didn't I think this through? I should have introduced them in small doses. Brought Lionel to the house for a few minutes and then worked our way up to an afternoon like this.

When we got close, my mom stepped forward toward Lionel like she was going to introduce herself. But my dad blocked her and got to Lionel first. He threw his arms around Lionel and gave him a huge hug. Lionel looked shocked. He hadn't been expecting it. I definitely hadn't been expecting it. I probably looked shocked, too. The gesture put my heart in my throat and tears in my eyes.

Of course, it was way too much, given that Lionel and I hadn't been dating long. "Um, Dad, we're dating. Save a little something in case things go really well."

Crap. I realized I'd just put the "m" word into everyone's mind without actually saying it. Although I'm sure my mom was already drifting in the direction of marriage, because that's what moms do. Oh, gosh. Then I looked at Lionel who'd managed to escape my dad's grip and he seemed fine. He wasn't running for the hills. He was standing there smiling uncomfortably at my family.

"Um, I brought these for during the game," Lionel

said, holding out the bag of pom-poms. "They're pom-poms. So we can cheer."

"Softball isn't really a cheerleader kind of sport," my dad said. Then he caught the look my mom was giving him. "Okay, it is now."

"That's so thoughtful of you, Lionel," she said.

"Do you know any cheers?" I asked him.

He got a panicked look on his face and said, "We're here, we're queer, get used to it?"

"Maddy, do you know any cheers?"

"I was never a cheerleader. I hated cheerleaders."

It was almost time for the game to start and there was one thing I wanted to do beforehand. What they cheered or if they cheered was something they were going to have to work out on their own.

I stepped over to my dad and said, "Could we talk for a minute, Dad?"

"Okay," he said, with a suspicious look.

We stepped a few feet away. "Listen, there's something I want to say. When I came out to you, you said I wasn't a man anymore—"

He frowned. "Oh, don't pay any attention to that. I just never thought..."

"It's an important question, though. What makes a man, Dad?"

He looked at me funny. "You know what makes a man. A man does the right thing by the people he cares about. A man takes care his family, his friends. A man stands up for people who need to be stood up for."

"See, I do all those things. And I know how to be a man because you taught me how to be a man. And that hasn't changed. That's never going to change."

"So I'm not in trouble?"

"No, Dad, you're not in trouble."

"I promised your mother I'd do better."

"You're doing great. Just relax, okay?"

"Okay."

"I know this has been hard and I appreciate you stepping up to the plate."

We both smiled at my timely metaphor.

"Speaking of which, you need to go play ball."

I waved a good-bye at Lionel and my family, and ran over to join the team. We turned in our roster and our lineup, and then took the field. The Limey Boys from The Pub were first at bat. Tim was our starting pitcher. Linda Sue was our new short stop, wearing a nice, short skirt that matched our jerseys. His wife had made it for him. In addition to my family, there were quite a few spectators, including Linda Sue's wife out there somewhere.

It was in the third inning that things started to turn around for us. The score was two to one in favor of The Limey Boys. Fetch had been walked, Tim had struck out, so had Simon. Linda Sue had hit a double, so there were runners on second and third, with one out left. So there was a little pressure on me when I stepped up to home plate. And not a little embarrassment, since I could hear Lionel cheering in the bleachers.

"We're here, we're queer, get used to it…" I couldn't believe he was going with that. Then I heard Maddy joining him. I glanced over and saw my mother standing up shaking a set of pom-poms. She poked my dad and he reluctantly stood up. They started the cheer again. All of them. Including Arthur, who was definitely not the sort to shout. That earned him a kiss on the side of his face from my sister, surprising both him and me.

"We're here, we're queer…"

It was distracting and energizing at the same time. I tried to focus. Raised my bat. The pitcher wound up and tossed the ball at me. The ball looked like it was coming toward me in just the right spot, so I decided to take a chance and swing.

And then, I hit a home run.

Also by Marshall Thornton

Boystown: Three Nick Nowak Mysteries

Boystown 2: Three More Nick Nowak Mysteries

Boystown 3: Two Nick Nowak Novellas

Boystown 4: A Time For Secrets

Boystown 5: Murder Book

Boystown 6: From The Ashes

Boystown 7: Bloodlines

Boystown 8: The Lies That Bind

Boystown 9: Lucky Days

Desert Run

Full Release

The Perils of Praline

The Ghost Slept Over

My Favorite Uncle

Made in the USA
Charleston, SC
10 December 2016